You Are My Fireworks

STORIES AND POEMS

PETE SCHULTE

YOU ARE MY FIREWORKS
STORIES AND POEMS

Author photo credit: Kathleen Schmidt

iUniverse books may be ordered through booksellers or by contacting:

iUniverse
1663 Liberty Drive
Bloomington, IN 47403
www.iuniverse.com
1-800-Authors (1-800-288-4677)

ISBN: 978-1-5320-8061-6 (sc)
ISBN: 978-1-5320-8062-3 (e)

Print information available on the last page.

iUniverse rev. date: 08/22/2019

You Are My Fireworks

It was the Fourth of July and late afternoon. Keswick was the lone cashier in the near empty grocery store. The deli was already shut down, so all you could buy was the usual junk. Keswick was just putting in his time, doing time really. At nightfall he'd walk back to his little apartment. Fireworks would explode in the sky. He didn't care a whiff. "What if everything just stopped?" thought Keswick. "What if I stopped? Everything stops eventually. Why not me, why not now? Okay, I'm just going to stop." And Keswick did stop …momentarily. But that's not the way life works — especially in a retail establishment. You can stop all you want, but they're going to keep coming. Oh yes they are. And they're coming, always coming…for you!

Magilicuddy was a tiny old man who moved at a snail's pace. Keswick spotted Magilicuddy and Magilicuddy spotted Keswick. "Please don't ask me any stupid questions," thought Keswick as Magilicuddy made a beeline for his register. "Dear God — or Jesus — or whoever the fuck is in charge up there. Please don't let this old man ask me any stupid questions. I just want to go home. Is that so wrong? Is it so wrong to want to be done with this and to go home? I ask you, creator person. You're home, I gather. Can't I do the same? Can't I just go home? He's going to ask of me something stupid, isn't he?"

Magilicuddy smiled brightly as he approached and regarded Keswick. He bowed to him. He tipped his cap. Keswick knew by now to remain silent, to let the customer do the work. Would he ask for change? Would he ask to use the phone? Perhaps it was directions to the restroom? Keswick knew enough by now to be dispassionate at all times.

Magilicuddy said to him, "Sir, I would like for you to get me some aftershave."

Keswick remained stone-faced. "You'll find the aftershave on aisle 9, sir."

"You don't understand," said Magilicuddy. "I wish for you to get it for me please."

"Look, buddy," said Keswick, "there's several different brands at several different prices. I don't know what you want or need. Just go to aisle 9 and pick something out."

"No, I can't go," said Magilicuddy. "You must go."

"I'm not going anywhere," said Keswick. "I can't leave my post. You go."

"No, you must go," said Magilicuddy. "I can't go. You see, I'm shot."

"You're shot?" said an exasperated Keswick. "Are you kidding me? Should I maybe call the cops?"

"No, no police," said Magilicuddy. "I just need some aftershave. Could you go please?"

"If you're shot," said Keswick, "then what the hell do you need aftershave for? You've got bigger problems."

"Hey, I like to smell good on any occasion," said Magilicuddy. "Now you go."

"Oh, for God's sake!" said Keswick, heading at a brisk pace for aisle 9 while muttering under his breath the whole way. "I can't believe I have fetch this guy aftershave. What does he need aftershave for anyway? Does he have a hot date or something? And this stuff about him being shot. What a bunch of hooey is that? Can't somebody shoot me? Put me out of my misery? I'll just grab the first aftershave I see. My time is valuable. Can't he see that? Bad things happen if you leave your post. I don't want bad things to happen. Does anybody? But they still do, don't they? Stay at your post. You'll see, bad things will happen anyway. It's the Fourth of July. Everybody's happy, right? Then some chum blows his thumb off. What's the good in that? So here I am, picking out aftershave for some tumbleweed who thinks he's got a bullet in him. I'll find him some aftershave all right."

Keswick grabble the first bottle he laid eyes on, a product called 'Brobus.' On the way back to his post he railed on about the damn Communists, the pot-smoking hippies, the boy teens who won't pull up their pants, the girl teens with their nose rings and tramp stamps, the latte drinkers, the distracted drivers, and all the managers he's ever worked for. Then, back at his register, he regarded Magilicuddy with irritation and placed the bottle in his hands.

"What's this?" asked Magilicuddy, sniffing the top of the black bottle. "I don't know what this is."

"It's Brobus," replied Keswick. "All the guys are using it. Go ahead, splash it on."

"No, I won't do it," said Magilicuddy. "I want something manly, but not overpowering."

"Look old man, you weigh a hundred pounds soaking wet. Nobody's ever going to accuse you of being overpowering."

"No, this won't do at all," Magilicuddy stomped. "I don't want this Brobus. Go get me something else. Something a bit more subtle. I trust you."

"Oh my stars!" exclaimed Keswick. "Now I have to fetch you something else?"

"You must!" stated Magilicuddy.

Keswick mumbled and grumbled and cursed, but back to aisle nine he went. This time he picked out a brand called *Sandlewood Dream*. When he returned to Magilicuddy, the old man greeted him with a warm smile. "Now what have you got for me? Something nice I hope."

Keswick passed the aftershave to Magillicuddy. "It's sandlewood. Manly yes — but not too manly."

Magilicuddy opened the cap and took a whiff. He smiled and nodded. "Yes, this is the one, this is it. I like this Sandlewood Dream."

"Good for you," replied Keswick. "We done then?"

"Well…"

"Oh boy," said Keswick. "Here we go."

"You see," said Magilicuddy, "I'm afraid I have no money to pay you, not a dime to my name."

"Of course you don't," said Keswick, resigned. "Of course you don't…"

"But I've something better," replied Magilicuddy, "something much more valuable than a few trifling coins."

"Go on old man…"

"I'd like to give you a big kiss," said Magilicuddy to Keswick.

"Are you crazy? I don't let perfect strangers kiss me."

"What about not so perfect strangers?" asked Magilicuddy.

"No way, old man. I don't want your slobber on me."

"How about a hug then?"

Keswick thought about it. "Oh, okay. It is a holiday after all. What harm is there in a little hug?"

"No harm," said Magilicuddy. "There is no harm at all."

The two men approached each other cautiously. Keswick leaned down while Magilicuddy looked up. They wrapped their arms around each other and awkwardly embraced. Keswick soon found himself patting Magilicuddy lightly on the back as if to say *enough is enough.* Magilicuddy, however, had other ideas and held tight. Then Keswick stopped patting and felt himself give in to something he didn't quite understand. He gave in, couldn't help but giving in, and then things inside him began building up, building up as if an eruption were about to occur, an eruption way beyond his control. It was petty bullshit that came up at first, that and more, so much more. Now it was cowardice and discontent, then mendacity, avarice, cruelty, jealousy, humiliations, failed relationships, regret, longing, sloth, anger, boredom, shame, missed opportunities, loneliness and time, all that wasted time he could never get back. It all welled up inside, flooding him. Then came the tears. They trickled at first, then fell down his cheeks in sweeping torrents. He could not stop them, he did not want to stop them. All this horrible stuff was leaving his body, gone. He found himself utterly forgiven, his body lighter than he'd ever felt in his life. Magilicuddy held Keswick close as the larger man continued to sob. "Remember my son, every day you're learning," Magilicuddy whispered into Keswick's ear. "Every single day. You are a good man, a decent man, everything I could have ever hoped for. You are my star, you are my fireworks, and you are my friend. I wish for you the happiest Fourth of July. I wish for you everything under the sun."

Magilicuddy broke the hug and Keswick immediately covered his face with his hands. He fell to his knees until his tears slowed and finally ceased. When he opened his eyes there was no old man, not another in sight. All that was left was a faint smell of sandlewood. Manly yes — but not overpowering.

January, 1986

The Centers for Disease Control reports that "The 1985/1986 influenza B epidemic that peaked in February 1986 was the largest influenza B epidemic in the United States since the 1968/1969 influenza season, caused by virus strains that were anti-genetically distinct from previous strains."

When I was a child I had a fever.
My hands felt like two balloons.
Now I got that feeling once again.

David Jon Gilmore/Roger Waters

He was sick so infrequently that it came as a total surprise when he was struck by the flu. Thinking back, it shouldn't have been any surprise at all. That said, the others in the house didn't even believe him at first, wondering whether his dull moans were mere artifice. They weren't. It was funny how fast the virus hit him. One moment he was listening to music. Was it Madonna's *Crazy for You?* Or maybe Bruce Springsteen's *I'm on Fire?* He'd like to remember it being Don Henley's *Boys of Summer.* That one he especially liked. But during that song or some other it felt to him as if he'd been clobbered by a sucker punch. But this sucker punch had come from within. It hit him and his head spun round and his body sunk itself into the couch. He could nothing but lie as still as possible, for any motion on his part would bring on waves of nausea and a sprint to the bathroom. He knew what it was instantly. He knew.

Upon reflection, he realizes that he was not as strong as he'd once thought. The flu had picked on an already weakened host. It could have killed him if it wanted to. It's interesting that nobody else in the house or those close to him became ill. He alone had to battle the flu bug. But just who was he, this young man in late January, 1986? I knew him well and I'll tell you about him. He was not yet 21. He'd left college voluntarily and without a diploma. He was working as a bellman at a hotel in one of the ugly, industrial parts of Florida that you don't see on any brochures. All of his bosses were horrible people, and the rest of the staff seemed just as miserable as he was. He remembers spending his lunch breaks in an empty stairwell. He began losing weight, and he didn't have much weight on him to begin with. And, some months prior, he'd managed to break his own heart. It's not that he had what you'd call low self-esteem, it's more accurate to say that he had *no* self-esteem. There was a book around that time called *Less Than Zero* by Brett Easton Ellis. He felt less than that — if that's even possible. But the worst part was that he felt there was no future for him. Even in his wild fever dreams there was nothing. He was a nobody and there was nothing and nobody for him. I guess you could say he'd hit bottom. But no. Because then, on his sick bed, on January 28th at 11:39 a.m., he watched in horror on television as the Space Shuttle Challenger blew up soon after lift-off killing all on board. He remembers clearly and misses those brave people to this day.

It was a colder than the usual January for Florida in 1986, and it turns out that the cold air may have contributed to the Challenger's demise. Florida is not supposed to be that cold, but sometimes it is anyway. The cold dips down from the east coast. What's to stop it?

So on further reflection, it appears that his immune system was indeed compromised despite a track record of robust health. He had given up on his education, stuck in a crummy job, had a sad heart, an unexplained weight loss (His buddy even teased him by calling him an anorexic motherfucker. Really, that bad?), and it was cold out there, the high for January 28 was 51.1 F, the low 30.2 F. Below freezing.

So he caught the flu and felt physically near death. His eyes bulged to red, watery slits, and it seemed even his skin and every hair on it ached and burned. But in reality, it was just an average flu, which infected an average person, which lasted about a week. Average. But his life was certainly buried in a hole, that's for sure. And like anybody else in that position he'd have to dig himself out. So, little by little (with plenty of bumps and hiccups along the way), I guess that's what he did.

The Growlers

"Yes, it's wonderful to hear your voice too, Marilyn. It's been so long. And yes, what you've heard is true. Frank did get laid off from the plant, and it certainly was unexpected. Twenty two years right down the drain. At first he wasn't handling it well at all. He was sleeping until noon and not showering or shaving. He was a total mess. At times he never got out of his pajamas and just watched television all day long and into the night. One day I caught him in the garage, day drinking, behind a giant pyramid of empty beer cans. I told him, 'Franklin, enough is enough. I won't have this nonsense in my house.' He just shrugged his shoulders and said, 'Okay.' Ever since then he's been a different man. He recycled all the beer cans and hasn't had a drop of alcohol since. Better still, he's been getting up before dawn every day and working out in the gym like a madman. Really, he cooks and does the dishes as well. I don't have to lift a finger. The only thing he asks of me is to measure him."

"Measure him? In what way?"

"In all ways. I measure his biceps, his triceps, his pectorals, his calves and his quads. I even measure his waist and count his six-pack."

"Frank has a six-pack?"

"He does now. It's amazing. And you should see his legs."

"But Patricia, why he does he want his muscles measured?"

"Because, Marilyn, they keep growing. His arms were 14 inches, then 15, 16, and now 17 inches thick. He's massive. He even had me measure, you know, that."

"You measured *that*? Really?"

"I sure did. And do you know what, it's growing as well. Two inches more at least. It's unbelievable."

"Is that even possible, you know, at his age?"

"I'll answer that by saying this: I don't know and I don't care. I'm just in outer space. I'm over the moon."

"I guess you would be."

"He even had a job interview lately and asked the interviewer about flex time."

"Flexible time?"

"You would think that's what he meant, but he didn't. Frank wanted the employer to grant him 15 minutes per day to flex his muscles in the mirror. That's how he interpreted *flex time*."

"Did they go for it?"

"Oh no, we never heard from them again — or any of the others. So with nothing going on with the job search, instead he's been attending these sessions with a male only group called *The Growlers*. They meet up deep in the woods once a week."

"What do they do, these Growlers?"

"I don't know. He won't really say. I suppose they just howl at the moon and chase each other around the fire. A couple weeks ago he even brought one home. A nice looking guy. The two of them sat in silence in the living room until I eventually joined them. Seriously, not a word was spoken. It was as if a spooky fog filled the room. And then, well, one thing lead to another and…"

"You didn't!"

"I did! Well, we did. It was amazing. They treated my like I was Diana the Huntress or something. It went on for hours and then the other guy just up and left like it was nothing. Not one word was spoken. Just these strange animal sounds. Weird."

"Come to think of it, I don't think I've ever heard your husband speak. Does he speak?"

"Of course he speaks. I know he does. Just not lately. I know he had a strong opinion on one thing or another. I just can't remember what it was."

"Probably animal rights I would think. So what comes next?"

"I have no idea. He's been spending more and more time with the Growlers. Sometimes he doesn't even come home. I swear, some day soon I'll see a wolf in the distance and that will be my Frank. Meanwhile, I hear they're building an underground lair to either fight crime or commit crime. I can't recall which."

"He's become otherworldly, a legend."

"My Frank, a werewolf. I thought I was making him howl, but it was really just the moon."

I Want to Be a Family Man

I want to be a family man.
I want to do just what I can.
Be there with the morning sun.
Be there when the day is done.
I want to be a family man.

I want to have a happy marriage.
I want to push the baby carriage.
Take care of business when I can.
Sleep at night when my race is ran.
I want to be a family man.

I want to bring the bacon home.
Stay away from where the ladies roam.
Keep my manners where they ought to be.
Working hard to build a family tree.
Yes I want to be a family man.

I want to fix the family car.
I want to be a movie star.
Try my hand at rodeo.

Steal a kiss at the picture show.
I want to be a family man.

I want to fix the water pipe.
I want to learn to do the Skype.
Share my pictures on the computer screen.
Eat some pork and then eat some beans.
Yes I want to be a family man.

I want to get my butt to work.
I want to see if I can twerk.
I'll do my workout maybe twice a week.
Let you beat me at hide and seek.
I want to be family man.

I want to give the good Lord thanks.
I want to fit into my Spanx.
Wash the dog and cook a meal.
Save a whale and save a seal.
Oh I want to be a family man.
Lord, just let me be a family man…

The Husbands of Madam Leftenright

One night, before going to sleep, Madam Leftenright's new husband, the suave Anatoly Nocturne, made an announcement. He told his wife that he no longer wanted to sleep in their bed. Since they just shared the most passionate of love, Madam Leftenright was rightfully baffled.

"Nocturne," she said, "why should you wish to leave our bed? I don't understand."

"I don't wish to leave our bed at all, my little dove. But rather than sleep on the bed with you, I wish to sleep under the bed beneath you."

"Why that's insane," said Madam Leftenright. "Who would do such a thing?"

"I would and I will," said Nocturne. "You see, I need the absolute darkness. I need the shadows and I need the quiet. I need to retire and I need to think."

With that, Nocturne rolled off the mattress and settled himself under the bed. At first Madam Leftenright was much dismayed. But then, stretching herself out on the bed, she didn't think the situation was all that bad. Nocturne still made appearances on the bed to share love with his wife. But he soon retreated to the closets, then the attics, then the basement, and then he was never seen at all. He had seemingly vanished.

One fine day an equestrian appeared on the scene. He jumped the fences, the shrubs, the fountain, and then, once invited inside, jumped Madam Leftenright herself. He'd introduced himself as Randy Luminaire. He was tall and blonde and beamed in the sun upon his mounted stallion. In time he proposed marriage to Madam Leftenright. "But I'm already married to Anatoly Nocturne," she protested.

"But where is this Noctrune then?" asked Luminaire. "I don't see him. Do you see him? We will go to see the judge. How can anyone expect you to be married to a man who isn't here?"

Madam Leftenright agreed. She'd fallen in love with Luminaire and wanted to be married to him instead. The couple soon met with Judge Flubert and pleaded their case.

"Madam Leftenright, how can I let you marry Luminaire?" asked the judge. "You're already married to Nocturne."

"But he's gone," said Madam Leftenright. "He must be. I tell you, I haven't seen him for ages."

"But what if he's to return? I would be made a fool of."

"Judge Flubert," said the Madam, "you remember when long ago we too were once lovers. If Nocturne were really alive, don't you think he would be in my bed where a husband belongs?"

"I do remember well," admitted the judge, "and it is the same now as it once was. I can deny you nothing, my dear. You are forever in my heart. As judge, I declare Nocturne a dead man. You are free to marry Luminaire. I only wish it were I."

The two lovers rejoiced and soon married. Luminaire jumped his new bride with great frequency and all was well with Madam Leftenright. But one night, midnight precisely, with Luminaire spent and slumbered by her side, a dark figure in a cape appeared at the end of the bed. It was none other than Anatoly Nocturne.

"Madam Leftenright," stated Nocturne, "there is another man sharing our bed. What is the meaning of this?"

"Nocturne, where have you been? I gave up on you long ago and married another."

"But I've been here all along," Nocturne replied. "As I told you, it was necessary that I retreat into the shadows for a time."

"Oh Nocturne, how can a woman expect to be married to a shadow? Look at Luminaire. He may be a man of leisure, a towheaded dandy in jodhpurs, but at least he's a real man, certainly not some sulking silhouette lurking in the cellar."

"Regardless, your legitimate husband has returned, and I insist this imposter leave our bed."

"Never!" screamed Madam Leftenright.

But Nocturne persisted. He proposed that he and Luminaire engage in a duel, the winner becoming the one true husband of Madam Leftenright. Luminaire agreed — with one caveat. "I will duel with you, Nocturne, unless you are a vampire. I admit that I am very afraid of vampires. Please state that you are not a vampire."

"While I may be dark, brooding, and covet the night, I assure you that I am not now, nor have ever been, a vampire. We shall duel at dawn, dear Luminaire."

The next day were gathered Madam Leftenright, Judge Flubert, Nocturne and Luminaire. Neither of their guns fired so they were forced to duel at close quarters. Nocturne was thought to be the favored, but Luminaire put up quite surprising of a fight. Their fisticuffs lasted until near noon, when an exhausted Luminaire finally became prostrate in defeat. Nocturne raised his hands in victory, but he too was thoroughly spent and dropped face first into the mud. Both men perished.

Later in the week, the gravedigger had nearly finished the task of burying the rivals side by side. He gazed up at Madam Leftenright when the last shovel of dirt had been cast. "Well, Madam, it appears that you're a single woman again."

"Don't get any ideas," Madam Leftenright curtly replied. "I'm through with husbands. If I want drama I'll go and see a play."

"Oh, I'm just a humble gardener, Madam Leftenright. Your station is well beyond the reach of a common man. But your fields do need tending to, and I'm plenty good enough for that."

"That they do, sir, that they do. Tell me, what's your name?"

"Gardener. Sam Gardener."

And so Madam Leftenright took on the gardener, Sam Gardener. And in the spring they planted, in the summer they danced, in the autumn they harvested, and in the winter they made love by fire light. The years went by as they should, and soon enough there was even the patter of little feet on the floor. They all lived happily ever after.

The Cleanest Guy in Town

Keswick and June often spent early evenings sitting on their front porch. Folks passed by at their leisure, waving a greeting to the couple over their white picket fence. One neighbor, Wallabee, caught their attention. It wasn't just his tall stature and dapper appearance that caused them to take pause. It was Wallabee's jolly whistling and the song he sang that always ended with the line *"I'm the cleanest guy in town!"*

"How do you like that Wallabee?" said Keswick to June. "Always bragging that he's the cleanest guy in town. Where does he get off?"

"He must be joking," June replied.

"Whatever do you mean?" said Keswick. "Look at those duds. Look at his hat. That get up must cost a thousand dollars easy. But he doesn't have to go on bragging."

June just laughed. "No, he *really* must be joking. I mean, that guy stinks to high heaven. He reeks."

"Reeks? But how can you tell? We're clear across the yard."

"Honey," replied June, "I'm six months pregnant. I can literally smell a stale cigarette butt from a country mile. For instance, I know you have a piece of licorice in your right front pocket as we speak."

"My gosh, I do!" said Keswick. "That's amazing."

The next evening, they heard Wallabee's merry whistling as he strutted down the lane. When he caught sight of Keswick and June he heartily sang out his signature line, *"Skiddily-diddly-doodily I'm the cleanest guy in town!"* At that, Keswick charged from his porch to confront Wallabee. Poor Wallabee was startled by Keswick's aggressiveness, but stood his ground, erect.

"Say, Wallabee, what's the big idea saying you're cleanest guy in town? Are you trying to crack wise?"

"No sir," replied Wallabee. "No sir. You see, in all my years I've washed behind my ears. That's why I'm…*the cleanest guy in town.*"

"I'm not buyin' it," said Keswick. "Something smells fishy."

"What's there not to buy?" said Wallabee. "Can't you see with your own eyes? Just look at me. Impeccable, stylish, one of a kindish. That's me — Wallabee!"

Keswick was unmoved. "Open your coat, Wallabee. I think I smell a rat."

"You smell no such thing, sir."

Keswick advanced and tore open Wallabee's coat. He sniffed as hard as he could, then retched and gagged. Composing himself, he said to Wallabee, "Jeez, you stink, man! What the hell?"

"I stink? No I do not. Why that's an affront, sir."

"It's no affront, Wallabee, it's a fact. You stink."

"But if my ears need soap, I scrub like a dope. That's why I'm…*the cleanest guy in town.*"

"Wallabee," said Keswick, "is it possible, just possible, that your *ears* are all that you clean?"

"Now why would I need to clean anything else? If my ears are spotless I could even go topless. That's why I'm…"

"No you're not, Wallabee, no you're not. You're dirty and you're stinky and I have no other choice than to make a citizen's arrest."

Keswick grabbed Wallabee and began pulling him into his yard. "Unhand me, sir, unhand me!" shouted Wallabee. Keswick called for June's help and they were soon able to pull Wallabee up to their porch. "June, we're gonna wash this dirty man. That's all there is to it."

"What country are we living in when you can just grab a man off the street and wash him?" questioned Wallabee.

"I'm afraid it's our civic duty," replied Keswick. "I do believe the country will thank us."

"Well," said Wallabee, "if it's your civic duty then I guess I'll have to abide."

"I'll fetch the wash tub," said June.

Keswick and June tried their best not to breath in the smell as they stripped Wallabee of his clothing. "Hey," said Wallabee, "what about my dignity?"

"We'll give you your dignity back after we've properly scrubbed the filth from you," Keswick replied.

"I sure hope so," said Wallabee, covering himself the best he could. "A man needs his dignity."

"Indeed he does," said Keswick. "Indeed he does."

In time, June returned to the toweled Wallabee with clothing fresh from the dryer. Wallabee quickly dressed, then checked himself in front of the mirror. "Well, Wallabee, how does it feel to *really* be the cleanest guy in town?" asked Keswick.

"I must say it feels just dandy. I've been cleaned from my head to my toes, and looky here, I smell just like a rose."

Wallabee trotted out the front door singing, "Dippity-dopity-doopity *I'm the cleanest guy in town…*"

The Namedroppers

Cornwallis and Lenny went to the same New Year's Eve party every year at Doug's house. They knew they could count on seeing a certain Ricardo Robbins in attendance. They knew Ricardo would be holding court, the center of attention of course, Mister six foot two and eyes of blue. Mister Namedropper. "So how long do you think it'll take Ricardo to mention his buddy, Pat Sajak?" said Cornwallis to Lenny.

"Oh, if it's anything like last year, probably ten minutes tops."

"How about we make a little wager then?" said Cornwallis.

"I'm up for a bet," replied Lenny. "You know me."

"I'll take the over if you'll take the under," said Cornwallis.

"Over ten minutes to mention Pat Sajak?" questioned Lenny. "No way. I'd be happy to take the under if you'll stick with the over."

"You're on!" said Cornwallis. "Loser does the dishes for the week."

After the wager was agreed upon, into Doug's house went the boys. Sure enough, they found Ricardo Robbins lingering near the shrimp bowl, casually popping one shrimp after another into his perfectly squared jaw. There he was, in all his six foot two glory, regaling two young lovelies about his days at sea. Cornwallis and Lenny were sickened. They didn't come to Doug's party to listen to Ricardo prattle on about responsible tanning, flexing on the bow, or paying lip service to saving the environment. They wanted to throw around some names — and they had a bet to settle.

The two lovelies were well-mannered indeed, allowing Cornwallis and Lenny to intrude upon their threesome. And after proper introductions were made, Cornwallis asked Ricardo if he was still working down at the depot. "Of course I am. Where else would a man want to work?"

"And I bet you even run into a few celebrities every now and then," hinted Lenny.

"Oh, from time to time I suppose," Ricardo admitted.

"Any in particular you'd care to mention?" continued Lenny.

"Not really," said Ricardo. "We're really quite busy most of the time. I hardly have a moment to notice such things."

Lenny wasn't buying it. "But if they happen to be on television most nights, surely you'd take notice — just a little."

"If Ricardo doesn't remember, he doesn't remember," injected Cornwallis. "But perhaps his recall will improve after eight or nine minutes go by."

"Say, what are you boys up to?" asked Ricardo. "Do you intend to make merry with me?"

"Heavens no," said Lenny. "Cornwallis and I just thought your two friends here would be interested in the people with whom you associate. I know I would."

"Yes, they might," added Cornwallis, "but only after seven minutes or so."

"I believe you do make merry with me," said Ricardo. "But if you wish to know that I've entertained the likes of Pat Sajak, then I'm fine with that. I have nothing to hide. Why, Pat and I…"

"I win!" blurted Lenny. "I win! He namedropped Pat Sajak. You're doing the dishes for a week, Cornwallis. Lather up, my little friend."

"You win nothing," Ricardo spat. "Nothing at all. You, Leonard, will never live as large as I. And do you know why? It's because you have no class, no style or panache. Had a person of Pat Sajak's esteem entered your establishment, you might well sell him a pack of gum, but then ask if he'd like to buy a vowel as well. As if he'd never heard that one before. And Leonard, I know for a fact that you crossed paths with Marilu Henner at a recent gala. And I know for a fact that after meeting Marilu Henner, you told her that you'd heard she was pretty smart in real life for a dame — *a dame*?! Oh, I heard she was as gracious as you'd expect from someone on television, but then turned to her companion and asked if anyone knew who that *rube* was. And you, Cornwallis? Don't look so imperious. I know that you've been bragging all over town about meeting not one but two cast members from tv's *Seventh Heaven*. But you couldn't let it end there, could you? I heard you started peppering them

— badgering them really — with questions about Beverley Mitchell, what's she really like and all that. They finally had to give you the brush off, saying in effect, *Hey dude, we're just actors, okay? Let it go. Have another drink.* See, you two losers will never know what it's like to be comfortable with celebrities, what it's like to be on their level. What I did with Pat Sajak was simple. I would bottle it if I could. See, I run into him and all he gets out of me is a friendly head nod and a slight smile of recognition. After that, you know, a trust is developed. Soon we're pals. But you guys, you fuck it all up. Pardon my French, but I can't say it any different. You fuck it up. You're fuck ups."

"Okay," said a dejected Lenny, "I can see we have different approaches. But tell us, Ricardo, what other celebrities have you seen lately?"

Ricardo thought it over, though this was mostly for effect. "Why, just the other day I made the acquaintance of one Juliette Lewis."

"Juliette Lewis!" said an excited Cornwallis. "Wow. Did you ask her about DeNiro, Scorcese?"

"Did you not listen to anything I've told you?" asked Ricardo. "No, of course you didn't. But I tell you, I gave Juliette nothing more than I gave to Pat Sajak. But mark my words, the next time I check my e-mail the very first name I'll see in my in-box will be…"

"Juliette Lewis!" cried Cornwallis and Lenny in unison.

"Exactly," replied Ricardo. "Exactly."

Happiness

Where does it go, this happiness?
Do you see it in others, their happiness?
Are you so sure about…happiness?

What are you doing with your happiness?
Do you have any to spare for others, this happiness?
Can I save it somewhere secret, happiness?
Is it something that will leave me, happiness?

Is it in a bottle, do you need to drink more?
Is it in your drugs, chemicals in your core.
Happiness, is it physical perfection?
Happiness, is it a flawless complexion?
Happiness, is it a spiritual direction?
Happiness, is it what you thought it was,
a tight-fisted Santa Claus?
Happiness.

Happiness, is it just around the block?
Happiness, in turning back the clock.
Give me some happiness
and I'll repay you tomorrow.

Give me some happiness
to ward off the sorrow.
Give me,
give me,
and I'll force a smile.

Where are you…happiness?
Where are you?

The Last Chance Lover
and the Kissing Bandit

Ramon, the dating expert, was doing his best to counsel Arturo, who sought help because his love life was a zero, had always been a zero. Ramon was under contract to provide for Arturo ten dates, one of which had to have at least some degree of success — meaning at least a second date or a romantic encounter. Failing that, Arturo's money was to be refunded. Thus far, nine dates had failed miserably and Arturo was down to his last one. Ramon had just one girl left for him, and this girl's record as far as dating was concerned was no better than Arturo's. Her name was Penelope, and Ramon described her to Arturo as thus: "She's got some cans, man. This much I can tell you. Cans as big as…well…big cans."

"Cans, really?" replied Arturo.

"And stems too," added Ramon. "Stems, gams, whatever you want to call them."

"Stems?" said Arturo. "She's got stems?"

"Like a dancer, you know?" said Ramon. "A ballet dancer with the long legs. And I'll tell you the best part…"

"It gets better?" asked Arturo, incredulously. "How can this be?"

"Of course it gets better," said Ramon. "For my favorite client I get nothing but the best girls. Let me tell you something, Arturo, this girl…this girl…well, she's got an ass that won't quit. That's the best part. That ass didn't quit today, it won't quit tomorrow, and it sure didn't quit yesterday. That's what I'm saying to you, my friend."

"She's got all this," said Arturo, "and you think she'd go for a guy like *me*? Is this even possible?"

"A guy like you?" replied Ramon. "Hell yes, a guy like you. You are Arturo Romero and nothing can stop you. Nothing. You are a red hot fire cracker!"

"Me? You really think so?"

"You just need a little back story," said Ramon. "Now work with me."

Ramon advised Arturo that he needed to add a little edge to his rather ordinary personality. He needed to learn to play a little hardball every once in a while, show everyone who was boss in this town. The ladies want that out of a man, Ramon counseled, they would respect his power and revel in his protection. By the end of their date he would have Penelope in the palm of his hand, *he would have her cans in the palms of his hands*. All he needed to do was to tell her this…

Arturo spied a girl sitting alone in a booth at the bar they'd agree upon for their date. She looked like a woman from a 1940's movie. Her dress was vintage, her lips bright red. She wore a red scarf over her hair. Arturo extended a single red rose as he approached the booth. "Might you be Penelope?"

"I just might be," she replied, taking the rose from his hand. "And are you the Latin lover I'm supposed to be meeting?"

"I certainly am," said Arturo. "May I take a seat?"

"Please do."

Arturo and Penelope shared pleasant small talk while enjoying drinks and appetizers. But Arturo had been this far along before, with nights like this ending with a simple handshake and some vague promises for a future date, which never materialized. It was time for him to play some hardball, just as Ramon had advised. "Before we go any further," said Arturo, "I have to come clean about something."

"Uh-oh," said Penelope, "here it comes."

"Hey," said Arturo, "I'm a hard guy and I have hard things to say."

"Say, I'm no easy dame either," Penelope replied. "Spill it."

"It's just that, well, I used to bang. In my past I used to bang a little. That's the truth of it."

"Bang on what?" asked Penelope. "Pots and pans on New Year's Eve?"

"No, that wasn't it."

"Bang on what?" she continued. "The drums? Are you a drummer in a band?"

"No, not that at all."

"Erasers?" asked Penelope. "Did you get detention and have to bang on erasers?"

"No," said Arturo, "nothing even close to that."

"Because that's what they used to do, before the modern day."

"I know that," said Arturo, "I do know that. But that's not what I'm talking about at all."

"Well, what are you banging on then?"

"I was in a gang, okay?" said Arturo. "I was a gang member. I banged with a gang because I was a *gang member*. Do you understand what I'm saying?"

"What kind of gang are we talking about here? Did you steal horses? Were you in a horse thieving gang?"

"A horse thieving gang?" said Arturo. "Are you kidding me? What is this, 1875?"

"Well how am I supposed to know?" replied Penelope. "What'd you do in this gang?"

"You know what a gang is, don't you?" asked Arturo. "You wear the certain colors, you stand on the corner and flash signs. That kind of stuff."

"What kind of signs?" asked Penelope. "Peace signs?"

"No, not peace signs," said Arturo. "Gang signs. With the fingers and the guns and the…"

"I like this one sign where aim your thumbs down and put your index fingers together. It makes a heart, see?"

"Oh brother," sighed Arturo. "this isn't working at all. I should quit."

"What's the matter?"

"Who am I kidding?" said Arturo. "I wasn't in a gang. That was just a ruse."

"So you didn't bang?

"No," he admitted to her, "I didn't bang. I was trying to play hardball with you. I was trying to get you interested in me. I meant no harm. I'm sorry."

"That's okay," said Penelope. "That's okay. So you didn't bang. You're still okay by me. But see, I have to come clean too. The truth is, though you may not have banged, I did."

"You?" said Arturo, exasperated. "You're telling me that *you banged*?"

"Well, just with myself. I was a gang of one."

"What's that supposed to mean?" asked Arturo. "You can't call it a gang if you're all by yourself."

"Well, I didn't need anybody else," said Penelope.

"What did you do?" said Arturo. "I won't tell anyone. I'm no snitch."

"I robbed a bank. That's what I did."

"What!"

Penelope told Arturo of a hot summer day, a yellow dusty kind of day without a single breeze to stir up the air. She was poor, jobless, with really nothing left to lose. On impulse she disguised herself beneath a scarf and robbed the first bank she came upon. Penelope managed to escape back to her apartment okay, but a dye pack the bank had inserted in her money bag exploded, discoloring much of the loot she'd scored. With the money she was able to salvage, Penelope bought a tandem bicycle at a pawn shop. She'd never even ridden it, never had a partner to ride with. "They call me *the Kissing Bandit*," she told Arturo, proudly. "I guess because of my bright red lipstick."

"You're the Kissing Bandit?" said Arturo. "I've heard of you. You're wanted. Did you know that?"

"Of course I know that," she replied. "But they probably don't want me all that much. I hardly got anything."

"Still, bank robbery is frowned upon."

Penelope agreed. She then had an idea. "Say, Arturo, how'd you like a second date?"

"A second date?" he replied. "Wow, that'd be new territory for me."

"Sure, a second date," said Penelope. "I'll break out my tandem bike. I'll sit up front, and you can ride in the back and flash gang signs at all your friends."

"I don't think I'd get shot to death for doing that, but more like ridiculed to death. I don't believe gang signs have ever been flashed from the back of a bicycle built for two."

"You can sit up front then," said Penelope. "I don't mind. I tell you, we'll have high times you and me. High times and big laughs."

So began a quaint courtship and eventually a life of crime for Arturo and the Kissing Bandit, although Arturo wasn't too impressed with the nickname the press had given to him. In bed, under the covers, he angrily shook the newspaper in his hands. "Do you know what they're calling us?" he asked Penelope.

"Who's calling us what?" said Penelope, absently filing her fingernails.

"Them, everyone, the police," said Arturo.

"What are they calling us, dear?"

"The Kissing Bandit and the *Oval-headed* Guy."

"So what's wrong with that?" asked Penelope.

"Well, every adult is more or less oval-headed," replied Arturo. "Is that the best description they could think of for me — the only description?"

"Hey mister," said Penelope, reaching for him under the covers. "I don't know about anybody else, but I like an oval-headed guy."

"But don't you understand that that isn't unique? Don't you get that?"

Penelope just laughed. Arturo wasn't much to look at, but he had in his bed the Kissing Bandit, and she wasn't going anywhere.

The end.

Postscript: The Kissing Bandit and the Oval-headed Guy are still on the loose. Who could ever arrest — or even suspect — a couple of hard core bank robbers on a bicycle built for two?

Bend it like Bigfoot

They were four best friends from Bend, Oregon, once boys but now grown men. Exactly twenty years ago, the boys went on a camping trip. Tony was the one who took the then famous but now pretty much forgotten photo of his three buddies. But it wasn't just a picture of three teenaged boys in a woody meadow. In the background, if you believe in such things, was Bigfoot, looking in on the scene from the tree line. They had no idea Bigfoot was in the picture until the photos were developed a week or so later. "Hey, what's that in background?" said Elvin to Walter, Daniel, and Tony. "Is that who I think it is?"

"It's fucking Bigfoot!" said Walter. "What the hell?"

After fighting amongst themselves for possession of the photo and nearly destroying it in the process, the picture finally landed in the newspaper with the headline: *Look Who Crashed the Picnic!* The headline infuriated the boys who never trusted the media again. "We weren't at a picnic," said Walter. "That was a hike. Ten miles at least." The boys were further humiliated at school when the other kids bastardized the headline to read: *Look Who Crashed the Tea Party!* The boys only trusted themselves after that.

Then of course there were the endless debates on whether what was in the background was really Bigfoot, or just a bear, a dog, a shadow, a tree, or a fake. Some yahoos came around and interviewed the boys, but nothing ever came of it except for the photo ending up in a couple phenomena magazines that catered to nerds and lonely old men. Tony, who took the darn photo, never even got any credit.

But, as written, this was twenty years ago. Times change, stories change, and boys become men. While drinking draft beers at Woody's Tavern, Daniel had the bright idea. "Why don't we do a reenactment?"

"A reenactment of what?" said Elvin.

"Of Tony's picture, of us with Bigfoot," said Daniel. "It's been twenty years. We should celebrate or something."

"That was some long hike though," said Walter, "at least twenty miles."

"Still, I'd be up for it," said Tony. "We could get the media involved — the right way. And I don't care if they call it a tea party. I play tea party with my daughter all the time."

"No, no media," said Daniel. "This is for us only. Let's make this about us, about four friends who've stuck together. What do you say, guys?"

After much debate and the clearing of schedules they all agreed to go. About a week later the guys found themselves trudging through the same woods from their youth. It was like a strange dream for all of them, where everything was the same only different somehow. All right, that was a dumb line but you know what I mean. The distances were shorter because their legs were longer, but they weren't in the same physical shape and had to stop and pee more frequently. Also, some of the woods weren't even woods anymore but housing developments and highways. Still, they pressed on and found themselves in the deeper and darker woods. Kind of spooky too in some parts, where you think someone's watching you, watching every step you take. Eventually though, they lucked upon the exact same location where Tony snapped the semi-famous picture. "Okay guys, line up," said Tony. "Let's get this done."

The guys did their best to remember who was standing where and what kinds of positions they were in. Before long they had it all set up, exactly as it was twenty years ago until…

"Hey guys, wait up!" said a voice from the woods. "You're not taking that picture without me."

After a moment of silence, it was Walter who broke the…well, repeated his line from long ago. "It's fucking Bigfoot! What the hell?"

They couldn't really see him exactly until he poked his head from between the thick branches. "Yeah, it's me, Bigfoot. I saw you guys coming up the hill and I really didn't think much of it. Then I put two and two together and thought 'Oh shit, those are my boys!' Do you believe it, twenty years? How fun is this?"

They all thought about running, but Bigfoot had such a friendly voice and certainly wasn't aggressive in any way. He just wanted his place in the photo. "I think I was standing here if I remember right," said Bigfoot."

"No," said Tony, "you were a little over there and to the right."

"Tony, that's Bigfoot you're talking to," whispered Daniel. "You don't give Bigfoot direction. If Bigfoot remembers doing a handstand, then let him do a handstand for God's sake."

"All right, all right," said Tony. "You're good, Bigfoot! Just hold steady there. Great! Got it! One more, okay?"

Tony got his reenactment shots and then Bigfoot called out and asked if he could approach. "You don't need to ask us," said Elvin. "We're in your house."

Bigfoot clamored over to the foursome. "Hey, who's got weed?" he asked.

"Not me," said Walter. "All I've got are some cough drops."

"Shit, you'd think I'd have some weed with all this vegetation out here," said Bigfoot. "But I don't. Sucks."

"We've got beer!" Daniel offered."

"Hey, good enough," replied Bigfoot.

The five of them set up a campfire and gathered round with their beers. There were a lot of questions to be asked, a lot of stories to be told, and many brewskies to drink. Tony looked at their gathered legs and feet and pointed out the obvious. "You certainly do have big feet, Bigfoot."

"Yes," he replied. "Hence the name."

"Have you ever eaten someone, Bigfoot?" Elvin asked.

"No, that's not my bag," he replied. "But we do need to eat, so you've got to do what you've got to do sometimes."

"I hear that, Bigfoot!" said Walter.

"We're an anomaly," continued Bigfoot. "Do you have any idea how good that is for the gene pool? Prevents disease of all kinds. I mean, all the good we do and do you know what we get? Jackass yahoos who hunt us down for pleasure."

"Not cool," said Daniel.

"If they ever caught us," said Bigfoot, "they'd put us in zoos, man. Of course, you'd get three squares a day but what the fuck? You've got to be free. You know what I mean? Let freedom ring, right?"

"I'm certainly down with that," said Tony.

After a lot of talk about kids and careers and aspirations and dreams and regrets and booze and this and that and the other, they finally had to call it a day. "Hey, let's meet again," said Bigfoot. "And next time we'll bring our families. If we all keep our mouths shut we can make it happen. I know we can."

The others agreed wholeheartedly and then Daniel spoke. "At the beginning of this trip I said we were four friends who've stuck together. But if circumstances were different, I really believe we'd be five friends."

"Circumstances be damned," said Bigfoot. "We are five friends! Five against the world! Now everybody put your hand in the middle."

Four hands filled the circle over the dying fire, and then one great big furry hand topped them off. "Here's to five friends!"

Rockin' Bob at the Birthday Party

Bob Romaine felt himself to be a lucky guy. It was the second year in a row that he'd been invited to a birthday party at the Cutter home. Mr. Cutter was Bob's boss, and it was always good to be close to the boss.

At the party's apex, the guests began gathering around the large dining room table in anticipation of singing the birthday song to the Cutter's five year old son. But just before the singing commenced, Mr. Cutter tugged Bob away from the table and the other guests. "Oh Bob," said Mr. Cutter, "I remember you telling me all about the exploits of your college band. What were you called again?"

"Yes sir, we were 'Rockin' Bob and the Bestie Boys.' Those were the days all right. My gosh those days…"

"Of course," said Mr. Cutter, "of course. Rockin' Bob and the Bestie Boys. Well, Rockin' Bob, I don't mean to insult you because I know you were in a band, a real band. But the thing is, this year we'd rather you didn't sing the Happy Birthday song along with the rest of us. Is that okay with you, Bob? Are you horribly insulted?"

"Certainly, Mr. Cutter, I won't sing. It's not a problem. But I'm afraid I don't understand."

"See Bob, the thing is, Mrs. Cutter is very particular about the Happy Birthday song. She — well, we really — thought your voice sounded a bit off at last year's party. It just didn't blend in as well as we'd hoped. Although we like you, Bob, as a person, we just don't appreciate your singing ability. Is that just an awful thing to say to somebody?"

"But sir, the child is only five years old. Do you think it really matters?"

"It matters to us, Bob. It certainly matters to us."

Mrs. Cutter tapped on the side of her glass with a spoon and made an announcement to the gathered revelers. "Before we begin to sing to young Chauncey, could we have all the non-singers retreat into the kitchen. Once again, all the non-singers please retreat to the kitchen. Thank you!"

Bob made his way into the spacious kitchen. He was joined by two others. They were children, a boy and a girl. "So you can't sing either," he said to the girl.

"It's not fair," she said. "I practiced months for this."

"You *practiced* singing Happy Birthday just for this party?" Bob inquired. "Are you kidding me?"

"Mother said to me, 'Arabella, if you practice every day, Mrs. Cutter will let you sing.' So I practice my guts out, sing a few bars for the lady, and I get banished to the kitchen. What gives?"

"So what's your story?" Bob asked of the little boy. "What's your name?"

"Stokley," the boy replied.

"So how'd you end up in the kitchen, Stokley?"

"You don't understand," mumbled Stokley. "I coulda' had class, I coulda' been a contender. I could have been somebody, instead of a bum, which is what I am."

Bob angered. "Listen to me, Stokley, you are not a bum, understand? You are not a bum. Hey, wait a second, were you just doing Marlon Brando from *On the Waterfront*?"

"So what if I was?"

"Nothing," said Bob, "nothing. It's just that you're, like, two years old. How do you know Brando?"

"I'm not two, I'm ten!" answered Stokley. "And I'm more into drama than voice. That's why I'm not that put out."

"Still."

The three non-singers listened grumpily as the others belted out Happy Birthday. "We should just leave," said Bob to Arabella and Stokley. "I'm so insulted. This is mortifying."

"I'm not leaving," said Stokley. "Mrs. Cutter said we can still have cake and ice cream even though we weren't allowed to sing. Don't you want cake and ice cream?"

"I don't care about cake and ice cream," replied Bob, fuming.

"Well that's a bad attitude," said Stokley.

"What about you Arabella?" asked Bob. "Aren't you at least miffed."

"Indeed I am miffed," she said. "But I can't leave without mother — and *she's* still out there singing. But I won't let this break me. I've still got a long career ahead of me."

"Jeez, these people," said Bob.

So Bob stayed on for cake and ice cream and decided to storm out right after that. But everybody else left after cake and ice cream so it wasn't much of a protest. He walked home.

Once inside his tiny apartment, Bob roused his bulldog, Robert, from a deep slumber. "Hey Robert, tell you what, I'll give you a cookie if you let me sing Happy Birthday to you. How about that?"

Robert wondered if it was indeed his birthday.

"I know it's not your birthday, buddy," said Bob, "but I've just got to sing to somebody."

When is my birthday anyway, Robert thought as Bob broke into the song. If I start howling and moaning will he be insulted? I'll just hold my tongue and hope he soon stops.

After Bob finished singing, he regarded Robert. "See, that wasn't so bad, was it?"

Well…

"Or did you just stay for the cookie?"

Well…

Robert thought about it after devouring the cookie. Hey, Bob, that was no night at the opera to be sure. That said, I've heard worse. You should hear that terrier down the hall. I mean what a yap on that little beast.

Bob cheered up as he gazed upon Robert's crumb-encrusted mug. "Happy birthday, my best buddy and bestest friend, happy birthday to you…"

Make Your Bed (The Musical!)

When the chickens rise and they need to be fed,
Yeah you, just make your bed.
When you're walkin' the streets and you need some cred,
Yeah you, just make your bed.

When your sheets are crumpled and your blanket is rumpled,
Yeah you, just make your bed.
When your brother's named Ted and your dog a big red,
Yeah you, just make your bed.

Hey, I'm just gonna sleep in it anyway…
The next day slips into the past.
Yeah, I'm just gonna muss it up anyway…
Tomorrow might be my last.
Now you tell me, why do I gotta make my bed?

But if you want to impress your lover,
And give a shout out to your mother,
Who told you, boy, just make your bed.

But if the pillows are jammin',
And the headboard keeps slammin',
Bright and early, I'll make my bed.

If your girl's named Polly
But she's crushin' on a Wally,
Then you, just make your bed.

If your boy's named Steven
And he's thinkin' hard on leavin',
Then you, just make your bed.

If your auntie's named Ella
And she's chasin' all the fellas,
Don't matter, just make your bed.

Make it now and make it good.
Bounce a quarter on it.
I knew you could.
Just make your bed — like you should.
Just make your bed — or sleep in the wood.
Yeah you, just make your bed.

Dirk Striker's Dream

Dirk confided to his wife, Cheri, about a recurring dream he was having. It was the one where he had an imminent test and he wasn't prepared. If he didn't pass the test he wouldn't graduate from Metro U. He wouldn't be a true Wildcat. What's more, he couldn't locate the classroom in a hallway where every room looked exactly the same. And to make matters worse, he was stark naked.

Cheri knew he was having nightmares because Dirk kept waking her with all his distressed thrashing about. "I wish you'd talked to somebody," she said to him. "You're driving us both crazy with these dreams."

"I am talking to somebody," Dirk replied. "I'm talking to you."

"But what do I know about anything? Talk to a professional."

Dirk made and kept an appointment with Dr. Rooter. He told Dr. Rooter everything he'd told to Cheri. "This is a fairly common dream you're having," said Dr. Rooter. "Most people can kind of just shake this one off, but you seem particularly bothered. I'd like to think it over and have you return next week."

Dirk returned the following week eager to hear the doctor's assessment. Dr. Rooter had a grave look upon his face. "I think, Mr. Striker, that the reason you're having these dreams is because you never did take that test, you never did graduate from Metro U."

"What?" said Dirk, aghast. "I most certainly did graduate. I have twenty different t-shirts, I go to all the games."

"So what?" said Dr. Rooter. "You can still wear the t-shirts. You can still attend the games. You can support the school any way you'd like."

"But I did graduate," protested Dirk. "I really did."

"Do you have a diploma?" asked the doctor. "If you do I'd really like to see it."

"Oh, I'll show you a diploma," said Dirk. "I'll show you."

"Because I did some research, and nobody by the name of Dirk Striker has ever graduated from Metro U."

Later that evening, Dirk and Cheri dug through their closets looking for the diploma. "Where are these damn diplomas?" asked Dirk. "Why don't we have them on the wall?"

"Because we're not nerds," said Cheri."

"Speak for yourself," said Dirk.

Dirk admitted to Dr. Rooter that he couldn't come up with his diploma but was sure it existed. For this session, Cheri joined her husband in the doctor's office. She spoke up for Dirk to Dr. Rooter. "I'm sure he went to Metro. I'm certain of it. Isn't that where we met, Dirk? Gosh, it was so long ago."

"No," Dirk admitted, "we met at a bar. Brooklyn's. You remember, Shakey was there?"

"Oh yeah," she replied. "Shakey."

Dr. Rooter dismissed Dirk from the office. He wanted to speak to Cheri alone. "I wanted to ask you about your wedding," said the doctor to Cheri.

"Yeah, what about it? We got married down in Pueblo."

"How many people attended?" asked the doctor.

"I'd say 50 or so."

"And how many came on behalf of Dirk?"

"Oh, I don't know," she said. "Shakey was there."

"And who exactly is *Shakey*, Dirk's brother?"

"No, not his brother. His friend."

"But no family?"

"No, no family," Cheri said to Dr. Rooter. "But he's from far away."

"How far?"

"At least as far as Florida."

"What are you saying?" questioned Dr. Rooter. "That's not even a straight answer. We're you ever *really* married?"

"I don't know," said Cheri, sobbing. "I don't know!"

"What kind of name is Dirk Striker anyway?"

"I don't know…"

"Do you even know this man?"

"I love him," whispered Cheri. "I love him. He's my little Buckeroo."

Dirk attended his next session with Dr. Rooter without Cheri. However, they were joined by a tall man with a dark suit. He introduced himself as Paul Aubry from the National Security Agency. After introductions were made and all got settled, Dr. Rooter spoke first. "Normally, Dirk, I wouldn't discuss your case with anybody else but your spouse. But I didn't see any other way of really helping you out unless I got some others involved."

"So you called the NSA?" said Dirk.

'Well, you'll see why," said the Doctor.

Paul Aubry lowered the dark shades he was wearing. "Mr. Striker, I'd like to discuss the biography you provided to Dr. Rooter."

"It's all true," protested Dirk. "I didn't tell any lies."

"I don't think you did either," said Paul Aubry. "But let me elaborate."

"Please."

"The high school you claimed you attended, St. Charles High, doesn't know you from Adam."

"What? You mean I never went to St. Charlie's? I was never a Blue Devil?"

"No, you weren't. And the middle school you mentioned, Riviera, doesn't exist anymore. It's condominiums now."

"Well, that's Florida for you," said Dirk.

"Same goes with your elementary school," said Paul. "It seems, Mr. Striker, that you don't exist at all. Never have."

"What?" questioned Dirk. "That doesn't make any sense at all."

"It didn't to us either," said Paul Aubry, "until we did a little more digging. It seems, Mr. Striker, that you were delivered to us long ago from one of our enemies. You were supposed to infiltrate and deliver unto them information that was very important to us. But something happened along the way. I don't know, maybe you were bonked on the head or something? Maybe you took too much cough syrup? But for whatever reason, our agency has determined that you don't know much of anything. In fact, we're all astonished at how little you do know — about any subject. Aside from being a good husband and a rabid Wildcats' fan, there's really nothing to you at all."

"I might take offense to that."

"It really doesn't matter," said Paul. "What's interesting is that somewhere along the line you created this man, this Dirk Striker, and somehow forged a life for yourself, made a complete break with your former self and the mission you were ordered to complete. For that we give you the utmost credit."

"Well," said Dirk, "thank you, I guess."

"The good news," said Paul, "is that for whatever reason your country wants you back. They've agreed to a prisoner swap with one of our people who was captured."

"I'm a prisoner?" asked Dirk.

"Right now you are," said Paul.

From a high train window at Denver's Union Station, Dirk said his final farewells to Cheri, who remained below on the platform. "Thanks for being my wife," he said to her, "if you really were my wife."

"Where are they taking you?" she asked. "What is your country anyway?"

"I don't know," said Dirk. "They won't tell me yet. I hope it's Italy though. That'd be a swell place for sure."

"If it's Italy you'll be getting a visitor real soon," she said to him. "I love you, I love you, I love you, Dirky-boy. You'll always be my little Buckeroo!"

The train began to pull away. Dirk said to her. "Good-bye, Wildcats! Good-bye, America! Good-bye, Cheri, my love. I'll miss you most of all…"

You Call That a Hokey-Pokey?

Holly is a Marketing Director for a start-up internet company. Her latest of endless meetings was held in the offices below Denver's Union Station. At the conclusion of the meeting she gathered her troops, ten new employees, in the crowded concourse of the train station. She thought it'd be great fun if the new employees did an impromptu Hokey-Pokey, which she would record for her bosses on her phone. The new staff moaned and groaned but went with Holly's instructions. They gathered in a circle and *'put their right hands in and pulled their right hands out'* and all the other movements the silly dance entailed.

"C'mon, everybody join in!" Holly shouted to the sparse crowd waiting for their trains. Two small children joined in but that was about it. Holly's Hokey-Pokey soon fizzled out with a few half-hearted claps. And that would have been the end of it if not for a grumpy old man seated not far from where the dance took place.

"This is a complete disgrace, Mabel," he grumbled to his companion.

"Now Horace, they're just having a bit of fun. Please settle down."

"I can't let this go, Mabel. You know I can't. It's an outrage is what it is."

"Horace, please don't make a scene."

But Horace could not remain in his seat. He stalked right up to Holly and raised his index finger to her face. "Missy, do you have the nerve to call what you just did a Hokey-Pokey? Do you have the nerve to do that?"

Holly slapped Horace's finger right out of the way. "Well that's what it was, buddy-boy."

"It's a damn disgrace is what it was," Horace countered.

"You bastard!" exclaimed Holly.

By this time Mabel had risen from her seat and got between Holly and Horace. "Wait a minute, Horace," she said, attempting to pacify her red-faced husband. "If these young peoples' Hokey-Pokey doesn't suit you, why don't you give it try with a group of your own?"

"Ha!" said Holly. "I'd like to see the old buzzard try."

"Oh, you'll see me try all right," said Horace. "You'll eat my dust, little lady."

Horace got right to it, dancing and prancing, shouting and cajoling, beseeching and screeching, anything to get people off their butts and into a righteous Hokey-Pokey. In just minutes he had the entire concourse, maybe 150 people, into a giant circle. Soon enough they had their *left elbows in and their left elbows out,* and all that jazz. It was an amazing sight that left Holly's mouth agape. But even she joined in. At the dance's conclusion people lined up to shake Horace's hand. They all congratulated him except for the last man in line. This man's face was stone cold. "Do you, sir, have the audacity, the daring, to call what just happened a Hokey-Pokey?"

"What else would you call it?" asked an out-of-breath Horace.

"I'd call it a Hokey-Jokey. That's what I'd call it."

"Do you want a fat lip right now?" said Horace. "Nobody insults my Hokey-Pokey and gets away with it."

"No," said the man. "I just want to show you what a real Hokey-Pokey is. You had some what, 200 people dancing? Ha, I slept with more women than that just last year."

"Okay, let's see you try it," said Horace. "But I don't believe you about sleeping with all those women."

"Well, after this Hokey-Pokey I'll get one yet. You bet I will. Hello, Hokey-Pokey. Good-bye, virginity!"

The man announced to the crowd at the concourse that his name was Herbie, and that they were to all follow him down the street to Coors Field if they wanted to participate in the world's largest Hokey-Pokey. With that, Herbie headed out of the concourse in the direction of the baseball stadium. Much to Holly and Horace's dismay, everyone in the concourse followed right behind him. It was as if Herbie was the Pied Piper of the Hokey-Pokey.

By the time Herbie walked the three blocks to Coors Field, there were over 200 people following behind him. A few more steps and they were at the gate. The ticket taker sized them up with an icy glare. "You have tickets to the game?" she asked Herbie.

"Absolutely not," he replied. "We've come here to do the Hokey-Pokey right in the middle of the baseball field. We'll need plenty of room. I do hope we won't be a bother."

"The Hokey-Pokey you say?" questioned the ticket taker. "Well, I guess that'd be okay. But hey, we'd better ask the umpire first. After all, there is a game going on. Say, mind if I tag along?"

"Not at all," said Herbie. "That's what we want. Bodies. Hundreds of them. No, thousands. Hey everybody, follow me into the stadium!"

With the gates flung open and abandoned, even more folks filed in behind Herbie. Maybe a thousand at this point. Who knows? In any case, Herbie steered his masses toward home plate and jumped up and down until he got the umpire's attention. "Hey there, blue, I'd like to call a time out."

"Now see here, mister," said the ump. "You can't call a time out. You're neither a player nor a coach. You're just…just…"

"I'm Herbie is who I am. And guess what? We're here to do a quick Hokey-Pokey. So if you'll be so kind to let us on the field for a moment, we'll be done in no time."

"Are you mad, sir?" the umpire asked.

"I am," said Herbie. "I'm mad for the Hokey-Pokey."

"You mean we should interrupt a televised Major League baseball game so that you and your gang can run out there and do the Hokey-Pokey?"

"It'll be great fun," assured Herbie. "I promise."

"Well, I guess I'll allow it," ruled the umpire. "It does sound like fun."

With that, the Rockies' star shortstop, Troy Tulowitzki, came charging over from his position to confront the umpire and Herbie. "What the devil is going on here?" asked Tulo. "Who are these people?"

"Tulo," said the umpire, "these folks want to come out onto the field and do the Hokey-Pokey. You don't mind, do you?"

"Jeez, I'm not sure," replied Tulo. "But hey, I like doing the Hokey-Pokey as much as the next guy. I'll get the players involved. Hey purple gang, let's do this thing!"

With the umpire and Tulo on board it was smooth sailing for Herbie and the gang. They all ran onto the field and took their places in a giant circle. Even the crowd in the stands got into it. There must have been 30,000 people strong in a mass Hokey-Pokey. It was pure heaven for Hokey-Pokey aficionados young and old alike. Everyone was thrilled with Herbie, climbing all over each other to congratulate him. Everyone, that is, except one guy… "Do you, sir, have the temerity, the gumption, the guts, to call what just occurred a Hokey-Pokey?"

"Of course I do," said Herbie. "Would you look at this crowd! That was the Hokey-Pokey of a lifetime. Thirty-thousand strong I might add."

"Ha," said the man. "This was nothing. I once had 30,000 people at my Bar-Mitzvah and I'm not even Jewish. Don't you think that I could beat your puny Hokey-Pokey?"

"If you can beat this Hokey-Pokey," said Herbie, "I will gladly shake your hand. But I can't say I believe you about the Bar-Mitzvah."

"Listen up, folks!" the man exclaimed. "My name is Herman, and I'm going to lead you in a real Hokey-Pokey. Follow me, sports fans, we're all going to Vegas!"

Herbie shook his head as he watched Herman leading thousands of excited Hokey-Pokey enthusiasts to Denver International Airport. He would fly them all that evening to Las Vegas. "It can't be done," muttered Herbie. "It just can't be done…"

But a few days later it was done. At the Las Vegas Motor Speedway, Herman led over 100,000 people in a raucous Hokey-Pokey that surely nobody could ever top. One woman in the crowd, however, wasn't so impressed. She sidled up to Herman and said, "You call that piece of crap, that pile of excrement, a Hokey-Pokey?"

"How dare you!" Herman exclaimed.

"Sir, my name is Helga, and I will take your lame-ass Hokey-Pokey and double it. Triple it, probably."

"You go, girl," said an impressed Herman to Helga.

And that, my friends, *'is what it's all about…'*

The end.

To note: The origin of the Hokey-Pokey is nebulous at best. One possibility suggests it came from an old-time ice cream vendor who sang out *"Hokey Pokey Penny a lump. Have a lick, make you jump!"* Now that must have been some swell ice cream.

Another theory suggests the dance derived from the traditional Catholic Latin Mass. The priest, with his back to the clergy, performs his sacred rituals. But all the clergy can see is him putting his left hand in, pulling his left hand out, grabbing at a chalice and shaking it about. It kind of makes sense when you think about it. My favorite version comes from Sheffield, England, published 1892.

'Can you dance looby looby,
Can you dance looby looby,
Can you dance looby looby,
All on a Friday night?

You put your left hand in,
And then you take it out.
And wag it, and wag it, and wag it,
Then turn and turn about.

I implore you to enjoy your Hokey-Pokey any way you like — looby looby. Next up, a startling expose on the Chicken Dance.

Target: Howard Marks

Kellen Conrad was still entry-level at the agency. He'd done nothing to esteem himself, but not given the chance either. His job was to look after retired workers with the agency, to make sure they still knew how to keep secrets following their tenure of service. This was important. They knew a lot, and could still do ample harm to the agency despite advancing age and circumstance.

To Kellen though, the position had plenty of downtime, weeks of unadulterated boredom. He often fell asleep at his desk. The retirees, after all, weren't all that active. They'd take walks, go to the park, the mall, and then eat an early bird supper. And that was on a busy day. Some days they'd just putz around in their underwear and do nothing at all.

But one day at the office there came a call with a tip. A double-agent, Boris Karkov, wanted Kellen to know that one of his possible charges, a Howard Marks, had chatted him up at the park and mentioned he'd worked on the *3.14 Project Series* back in the day. Karkov thought the old man knew what he was taking about, though he appeared confused at times and was possibly demented.

Kellen studied up on Howard Marks and the 3.14 and found most of the documents blackened out. This was serious stuff, he thought, serious enough to kick it upstairs to Mr. Smith. Not doing so would be risky. Though this was probably nothing, a mistake and the wrath of Mr. Smith could end his career, or worse.

That same afternoon, Kellen was let into Mr. Smith's office. He cautiously approached his intimidating boss. He was not invited to sit. "What have got, Conrad?" said Mr. Smith. "It'd better be important."

"I've got a former, sir," Kellen replied. "Howard Marks, age 91."

"Never heard of him."

"I did some checking," said Kellen. "He's in good physical health, this Marks, but mentally he's slipping. Perhaps symptoms of dementia."

"Keep going…"

"Anyway, Marks talked to my double, Karkov, in the park over a game of chess. It seems he mentioned something called the 3.14 Project Series. It sounded familiar to Karkov and he became concerned. What is the 3.14 anyway?"

"What that is, Conrad, is none of your concern. Understand?"

"Yes, sir."

"Now go about your business, okay Conrad? I'll call you if I need you."

With that, Kellen was dismissed from Mr. Smith's office and returned to his own. The call from Mr. Smith came within the hour. He was ordered to return at once. This time he was asked to take a seat. "Conrad," said Mr. Smith, "this is what you need to know. Marks must be terminated at once, and you're going to arrange for this to happen. With his advanced age and dementia, he cannot be trusted with information regarding the 3.14. The 3.14 still has repercussions to this day. Is that clear to you?"

"It is clear," replied Kellen, "but termination, sir? Is such an old man really that dangerous?"

"Now don't give me those puppy dog eyes, Conrad. Marks has lived a long life, a good life. But he signed on for this just like we did. Rule number one: If you spill the beans, the beans spill you. You have a problem with that, Conrad?"

"No, sir."

"Now your mission is to go to the West End Seniors Center. You will ask for Andy — no last name. When you make contact, you will inform Andy that there has been a breach. You will provide the name Howard Marks. That is all. Also, you will be in full disguise. This will be an in-person contact. No calls or computer, no trace at all. Clear?"

"Yes, sir."

"And Conrad," continued Mr. Smith, "you must not fail. Failure would be highly detrimental to the agency, and to you particularly. Got it?"

"Yes, sir. I've got it."

Kellen felt ridiculous in disguise. He never wore a ball cap and this one seemed to sit funny on his head. His glasses were too large for his face and his fake mustache made him look like a 70's era porn star. His limp felt forced and the artificial cast on his arm itched. He couldn't wait to get this over with.

After arriving at the West End Seniors Center, Kellen waded through walkers and wheel chairs to get to the reception desk. He'd given up on the limp already. He was met at the desk by a young women wearing some kind of nursing uniform. Her name tag read 'Paulette.'

Kellen Conrad had always thought himself too smart and cautious to believe in such a silly concept as *love at first sight*. That is, until he looked into the gray-green eyes of Paulette. Oh, he was smitten all right, but he had a job to do. He had to help kill an old man.

"May I help you?" asked Paulette.

Kellen didn't know whether to ask for Andy right off or poke around for him first. So he said to Paulette, "My parents are aging. I wanted to get a look at your establishment."

"Our establishment?"

"Well, I wanted to see if it was a nice place. That people are cared for."

Paulette thought for a moment, then said, "They are cared for here. I see to that. They're like family to us, all the way to the end. Would you like a tour?"

"Yes, that would be nice."

"But first," said Paulette, "you must tell me where you got those glasses. They're fantastic. You look like Elton John."

"Oh, thanks. My usual ones broke."

"Like you arm," she continued.

Kellen glanced down at his fake cast. "Yes, like my arm."

"What is you name anyway?"

"My name?" he said, buying some time to think of a good one.

"Yes, your name."

"My name…is Ben Sterling."

Paulette smiled and thrust out her hand for him to shake. "It's very nice to meet you, Ben Sterling."

Paulette's tour was thorough and very detailed, but Kellen wasn't listening to a word she was saying. Instead, all he could think about was wanting to hold her hand, wanting to kiss her lips, wanting her, loving her. It was the best tour he ever had, this tour of the old folks home. Then she came upon a room and poked her head in. "Mr. Marks, how are you feeling this morning?"

"Well, I'm not dead yet," he said from his bed, this tiny old man under the covers.

"No," laughed Paulette, "of course you're not dead. I'm afraid you're going to be with us for quite some time."

"Oh, don't tell me that," replied Howard Marks. "Please don't tell me that."

"Now, Mr. Marks, please don't joke around like that. I'm giving Mr. Sterling a tour, and we don't want to give him the wrong impression. This is a happy place."

"Sterling," said Howard Marks, "run — don't walk. That's all I'm saying. This one's beautiful, but I trust her about as far as I can throw her. The pretty ones are deadly."

"Oh, Mr. Marks," said Paulette, "you tease me so much."

They soon left his room and resumed the tour. When they got back to the desk, Paulette checked her watch and hinted to Kellen that their interaction was over. Kellen quickly gathered his senses. "I'm wondering, Paulette, if an acquaintance of mine is still working here. His name is Andy. Do you know him?"

"Andy? Of course. I'll call him in."

Andy came in and looked Kellen over warily. Kellen greeted him as if he were a long lost friend and did his best to find them a place out of earshot from the desk and Paulette. Satisfied, he whispered to Andy, "There's been a breach…"

It was well after midnight when Andy entered the room of Howard Marks. He found Howard, wide awake, sitting at his desk by the window. "You're still up?" inquired Andy.

"Yes," replied Howard. "I knew there was something screwy going on when I had two visitors today. That's two more than I've ever gotten."

"You mentioned the 3.14 to somebody at the park. You know you can't do that."

"I did?" said Howard. "Well, maybe I did. I can't keep track any longer. It's all so confusing."

"I know," said Andy. "That's why I'm here."

"Wait," replied Howard. "Before you do you worst, let me have one more drink — and you have one too, with me, for old time's sake."

"That's fine, Howard. One more drink."

"What will it be," asked Howard, pulling two bottles from the lower part of his desk, "whisky or gin?"

"Whiskey is fine," said Andy.

Howard poured two glasses and passed one of them to Andy. They toasted to good times and then it was down the hatch. Andy was fine for a moment and then felt something burning deep inside. Then he went to breath but couldn't without gasping. Then he knew he shouldn't have taken that drink.

"Why did you choose whiskey?" asked Howard. "Doesn't anyone drink gin anymore?"

Kellen got word that Andy was found dead. He had no choice but to give this information to Mr. Smith. Needless to say, he was not pleased. "Andy is dead? That fool. I should just hire senior citizens for these positions. Everyone thinks they're so stupid, and yet, look what happens? Marks is alive."

"I'm sorry, sir."

"You're sorry? Well, Conrad, I have no use for your sorrow. I need you to contact the one person who will not fail, the one person who has never failed. I need you make contact with… Paulette."

"Paulette?" questioned Kellen.

"Yes. Paulette."

It's Elementary (My Dear Watson)

There's doings on the moor
as there's been some kind of fright.
Seems the Hound of Baskervilles
is roaming in the night.
It's elementary.

This Sherlock Holmes, indeed, favors
a logical conclusion.
The fearsome hound, he knows,
may be a strange illusion.
It's elementary.

Oh…it's elementary!
It's elementary.
Dear Dr. Watson…
It's elementary!

The fiend needs no disguises,
does his deeds behind the scenes.
Now the cold and fog are seeping in
and he's getting kind of mean.
It's elementary.

Holmes and Dr. Watson raise
their guns and take their aim.
They better hope the roaring
Hound is just a little off his game.
It's elementary.

Oh…it's elementary!
It's elementary.
Dr. Watson…
It's elementary!

They chase the fiend into the night
engulfed in soggy bog.
The monster merely a man at best,
The Hound was just a dog.

It's elementary.
It's elementary.
My Dear Dr. Watson,
it's elementary.

Case closed.

I Only Want Soup:
A Valentine's Story

Young Petey was unceremoniously summoned to Mr. E's office, he the Principal of the school. Petey half expected it as he'd borne the brunt of his teacher's scorn. But he wasn't the only one. His classmate Michelle was waiting in the secretary's office as well. Petey was surprised to see her there. "What are *you* doing here?" he asked.

"I have to talk to Mr. E."

"So do I," said Petey. "Are you in trouble?"

"I think so," she replied. "Are you?"

"Seems so."

Mr. E thundered into the room from his office and gestured for the children to come in. They sat in little chairs in front of his desk. He towered over them from the other side. "You, Petey," said Mr. E, "do you know why you've been called into my office?"

"Because I only want soup."

"And you, Michelle?"

"I only eat salad."

"So," said Mr. E, "soup and salad. Is that what we have here? Tell me, Petey, what is it about soup that you like so much?"

"Oh, I like the way it tastes, and the way it fills up my tummy and makes my tummy warm. I like chicken noodle soup best of all. Sometimes I wish I could make myself shrink small, and I would jump into the bowl and swim with all the noodles. Oh, I love soup. I think about it often."

"So I hear. And you, Michelle, what is it about salad that you hold so dear?"

"I love lettuce even though my daddy says it hardly tastes like anything. And I put radishes on top, and cheese, and bacon bits, and peas, and corn, and sunflower seeds, and raisons, and celery, and eggs, and croutons, and dressing, and…"

"Thank you, Michelle," said Mr. E, cutting her off. "Thank you. Now children, what I want to talk to you today is about balance. And by that I mean I'd like you to mix up your diets a little. Say, instead of soup or salad, have pancakes for breakfast, perhaps a tuna sandwich for lunch, and a pot roast for dinner. You see, you can still eat well while not eating the same thing for every meal. Besides, what if your mommies forget to pack your lunch, and it turns out that the cafeteria is not offering soup or salad on that day? Why, you'll go hungry for the day and you won't grow. We can't have that. At this school we want to grow our minds and our bodies. Don't you want to grow bigger?"

Petey and Michelle both nodded their heads enthusiastically. They did want to grow. They wanted to thrive. They wanted all that life had to offer. Except…

"So, Petey," said Mr. E, "now they I've spoken my piece, is there anything you'd care to say for yourself?"

"I only want soup."

"Naturally. And you, Michelle?"

"I only eat salad."

"Of course you do," said Mr. E with a sigh. "Kids, I can tell from your youthful obstinacy that you're perfectly healthy despite your rather limited diets. You know, soup and salad, I know you're too young for this now, but somewhere down the line you should meet up again. You'd make a very nice couple."

They both blushed and shook their heads from side to side.

"You don't think so?"

"No, no, no," Michelle moaned. Petey looked at her and smiled.

Mr. E shook his head and dismissed the two from his office. While walking her back to class, Petey said to Michelle, "Do you think we'll ever meet again? I mean, when we're grown."

"Have you already turned seven?" she asked him.

"Yes. I had a birthday party but no girls were invited."

"See," she said, "you're much too old for me. I'm only just six. It would be impossible. There's really no future for us."

"Well," said Petey, "at least we can still be friends. Friends?"

"Yeah, shake on it."

And of course they did meet again when they were grown. And they did go to dinner. And we know just what they ordered.

The Cruel Spring and the Simple Passage of Time

It was late afternoon when I ducked into a bar I went to every now then. It was nothing fancy, just a place to have a beer or two if I had the time. I usually kept to myself and didn't see many familiar faces. But this day was different.

I recognized a guy sitting at the end of the bar and could see that he knew me as well. It was Randy Perkins. He was an old classmate a few years ahead of me. I gave a slight wave and reluctantly went down to meet him. "You didn't have to come over, Michael," he said to me right off. It was always difficult with Randy Perkins…

Since I did come over he glumly offered the barstool next to him. I glumly accepted it. "So, how are you, Randy?" I asked him.

"Very well. Hey, why don't I buy you a drink? You weren't so bad back then. You weren't so good either, but hey, I'll still buy you a drink."

"Thanks, Randy."

Randy Perkins was known those years ago as a skinny oddball freak who dared to be different when being different could get you hurt. The other older kids had it in for him, a seething hatred and were just looking for an excuse. One day he gave them one.

I was hanging out with my buddies, a loose circle of gangly legs on rusted bikes. Spring was everywhere but we hardly noticed. Just the usual bored teenagers. And then there he was, Jeremiah Roop, riding up to us in breakneck speed before skidding to a halt. "Hey guys, guess what? The big kids caught Perkins in the park! He was picking flowers without his pants on. They've got him cornered. Let's go!"

We raced to the park as fast as we could pedal. A guy caught picking flowers without his pants on? That was good stuff for bored kids. At the park we stopped and listened for any commotion in the dense brush. Finally we heard random shouts and laughter and found the older kids surrounding a large oak tree deep within the park. We quietly gathered behind the others and searched the giant oak for any sign of Randy. Sure enough he was up there, bare-assed as described by Jeremiah. "Get down here now, Perkins!" yelled Tony Crane, their tough guy leader. "Take your punishment!"

"Leave me alone!" Randy hollered back.

"Down here!" Tony commanded. "I'm afraid your flower picking days are over."

Randy didn't budge, and it wasn't long before rocks and dirt clods started flying up to his perch within the branches. He didn't last long. We listened as the sick thud of rocks struck his paper-thin body, and suddenly branches were splitting and Randy Perkins landed with a hard thump on the ground. He didn't move a muscle, half of him naked and covered with welts and blood. We all thought he was dead. The older kids scattered without a word and so did we. It was Jeremiah Roop who finally stopped us from fleeing the scene. "Wait," he said. "We can't leave him like that. Let's find some grown-ups. Let's get him some help."

With Jeremiah leading the way, we eventually found some construction guys to tell, and not long after we heard the sirens begin to wail. Help was on the way for Randy Perkins, and here I probably would have just pedaled away with the others if not for Jerry Roop. It hurt to face him, this Randy Perkins. It always did. "Randy," I said to him, "how did you come back from all that?"

"From all what?"

"You know, the thing in the park...with the flower picking and the tree."

"Oh, that," he said. "Well, it was hard at first, especially the next few days at school."

Randy Perkins was back in school the very next day after his fall from the tree. In those days you didn't miss much school — for any reason. Kids would come by your house, and if you weren't projectile vomiting or bleeding profusely from the anus, you went to school. The thought was, *if I have to get my ass to school, then your ass is going to be there as well.*

"But you know, Michael, the best thing to happen after the tree thing was the simple passage of time. Other things happen in life. The world spins on. I mean, it was big news when you yourself took those pills and went down. It was big news…for about a week. Then we all went on our way. It's sad to think about it like that, so you just stop thinking about it at all."

"But what about you, Randy? Here you've done so well for yourself. I want to follow your example. You don't seem to let the past creep in at all."

"Michael, I will tell you this: I still love to pick flowers, and for that matter I like not wearing any pants. And anyone who has a problem with that can kiss my mother-fucking ass. How's that for burying the past?"

It's Just the Moon

They were traveling back to earth in their shuttle, the Lunastrata. They had no passengers, only cargo. Tourist travel to the moon had dried up thanks to the opening of Mars. Moon novelty had worn off months ago. After the taking in the view and doing some shopping, there really wasn't much to do up there. So they were coming home, for the last time, or at least until they could catch on with a Mars shuttle. One pilot didn't mind so much. For the other though, it was devastating. You see, he loved the pilot sitting next to him. He loved their time on the moon, so far away from the headaches back on earth. Oh to be on the moon again, he thought, in their little room with a view of deep space, a billion stars shimmering, shooting stars they could almost reach out and catch.

Pilot Colten Rahway was married. Well, sort of. His wife Debbie left him after 'Seeing the Light.' This was the new thing to do on earth. If you wanted permanent happiness, all you had to do was go into a room and stare at this special light for 30 minutes. That was it. Permanent happiness. Everyone was doing it. Which was fine for Debbie, but she said to Colten, "How can I be married to you or anyone else when I'm now married to the universe?" The entire universe. How could he compete with that? So Debbie left him and everything else in her life. She was off painting the world with other happy people, painting one another or some other kind of hippy shit. Colten didn't even know if he had a home to return to. These blissed out people just left everything behind.

Pilot Sarah Jackson was also married, happily enough except for the moon affair with Colten. She had a husband named Steve and two small children. Pilot Sarah Jackson thought, "We're only halfway home. I'm going to give this pilot next to me the best backseat sex of his life, if only he'd knock off the sad sack routine." Pilot Sarah Jackson did not tolerate melancholy. She was upbeat and excited about returning home.

"I wish we could turn around and go back," said Colten.

"Are you kidding me?" replied Sarah. "There's nothing left up there but some mining. It's over for the moon."

"But we had each other," he said. "I guess that's what I'll really miss."

"Remember what I told you, and what we agreed upon? When this is over, we're over. You got it? I have babies at home. I have a husband."

"But I love you," said Colten. "I didn't want to love you but I was lonely. I wanted your companionship and yes, your sex. But here I am in the middle of outer space and I love you so much. You're my kitten."

"Look," she replied, "if things were different. If things were different, but they're not. They're not different. There are certain facts about this life. We talked about this and you said you understood."

"I know. I know."

Sarah held his hand and then leaned over and kissed him. Then she took him into what constituted the backseat and rocked his world, or whatever world or in between world they were currently in. Afterwards, their bodies spent but still intertwined, Colten harkened back to the moon. Always back to the moon. "I love this view of the moon," he'd said to Sarah after one of their couplings, she face down on the bed.

"What are you talking about?" she'd replied. "It's just dull gray with ragged edges."

"I was talking about your butt."

"Oh, that's funny," she'd replied, but didn't laugh at all.

Colten considered that Debby always laughed at his jokes even when they weren't all that funny. But Debby left him. So Sarah never laughed. Perhaps he should be with someone more serious-minded? Sarah looked over at Colten, as if reading his mind. "You know, when I get home I'm going to *See the Light*. We all are, Steve and the kids."

"No," said Colten. "That's awful. Don't do it."

"Why not?" she replied. "Don't you want to be permanently happy? There are no side effects. There's no downside."

"I don't trust it."

"Come on, Colten. Just see the light. Then you wouldn't be such a grumpy grump and a sippy sap."

"I'm not a grumpy grump. I'm the happiest I've ever been. I mean, look at us. We're stark naked in outer space. We just had cosmic sex. Nothing touches us."

"It will," she said, "when we get home."

"I think though, when I get extremely happy I get careless, I make mistakes. As a pilot, you can't make mistakes. You know that."

"But I think," said Sarah, "that if you're both competent and confident you won't make mistakes. And if I can be happy all the while…"

"It's too good to be true."

"Grumpy grump," said Sarah.

After they landed safely at the space port in Denver, Colten was ready for his famous final scene with Sarah, his big good-bye, their last soft kiss. Then he saw big Steve and the kids bounding up the shuttle, their faces beaming, their arms extended, awaiting hugs from their mother, Pilot Sarah Jackson. All Colten could manage was a faint wave, which she returned, more faintly then his own.

Colten drove back to his home but somebody else was living there. He tried asking about Debby but the person at the door was making no sense at all. They sure were happy though. Colten was certain that they'd *seen the light*. He ended up checking into a hotel where he'd stay a few days to gather his thoughts, to plan his next move.

In the daylight hours he found a park that he liked, where he walked for miles and sat in the sun. He thought about Sarah and the domestic life she so easily returned to. He had nothing but a memory of her and that had to be enough. "When this is, we're over," she'd said to him and meant it. Colten turned his gaze to the mountains. He didn't expect it but there it was, the moon. It was full and steady and hung high above the broad peaks. He gazed at it and couldn't remove his eyes. He was entranced. How many times had be been to the moon? Yet still entranced. Another walker ambled up and took notice of Colten's fixation. "Hey, buddy, what are you lookin' at? It's just the moon."

Colten snapped out of his reverie and regarded the man before him. "Yeah," he said with a shrug, "it's just the moon."

**Coming soon…Colten goes to Mars.

We're All Going to Work

Who is it gonna work today?
Who is it got some bills to pay?
Who is it got some money to burn?
Who is it gonna spend what they earn?
That's you, man, that's you.
That's you, man, that's who.

Yeah, it's the lawyers and the politicos,
the window washer with a bloody nose.
We're all going work.
Yeah, yeah, we're all going to work.

It's the disco jockeys and the sleepy heads,
the hippies with their hemlock dreds.
We're all going to work,
Yeah, yeah, we're all going to work.

It's the book readers and the deep thinkers,
it's the beat riders and the day trippers.
We're all going to work.
Yeah, yeah, we're all going to work.

Who is it gonna take my job?
Who is it gonna set me free?
Whatever it is that I may be…
A night sweeper,
a day dreamer?
Who is it gonna take my job?
Who is it gonna set me free?
A rabbit runner,
a Vegas stunner?
Who is it gonna take my job?
Who is it gonna set me free?
Cloris Leachman?
A lady of distinction?

For it's the players and the sex machines,
the high-heeled junkies
and the promster queens.
We're all going to work.
Yeah, yeah, we're all going to work.

It's the killer jacks with bronzed guitars.
It's the muscle heads with cast iron bars.
We're all going to work.
Yeah, yeah, we're all going to work.

You say you don't wanna work today. Oh no!
You say you got another game to play. Oh no!
I don't wanna work!
No, I don't wanna work!
But that ain't the way it is, man.
That ain't the way it is.

For it's the cowboys and their lonely crew.
It's the pick up hustlers and the color blue.
We're all going to work.
Yeah, yeah, we're all going to work.

It's the dragon man and the kid with mice,
it's the wedding crasher with a packet of rice.
We're all going to work.
Yeah, yeah, we're all going to work.

It's the train ride back when your time is up.
At the end of the day you gotta feed the pup.
Hey, hey, we're all done with work.
Yeah, yeah, we're all done with work.

It's the bedside manner when they tuck you in.
It's a free ride to heaven if you didn't sin.
Hey, hey, we're all done with work.
That's right, we're all done with work.

The Noodle Bowl Incident

It was that window of time when many of his friends were having their first weddings. Lonny had been to several weddings during the year and here was another. Now it's the reception, now it's supposed to be fun, but he had business to attend to first. He'd kept running into his old high school chum, Lauren, at these things and tonight was no different. What Lonny needed to do was to get with Lauren early before she started talking shit about him. It was so embarrassing, being laughed at for something he didn't even do. Lonny was determined to clear up their misunderstanding once and for all. He found her admiring the wedding cake in the corner. He got her attention straight away. She wasn't going anywhere.

"Lauren, what a pleasure to see you again."

"Oh, Lonny, did you happen to drive here?" she asked.

"I did."

"Well, I hope you were careful this time."

"Yes, Lauren," said Lonnie, holding back his irritation. "I was very careful. In fact, driving is something I wanted to discuss with you before the party begins, before either of us has had anything to drink."

"Please," said Lauren. "Let us discuss."

"Lauren, it seems you've had some great fun at my expense these last few receptions relaying a story about you seeing me driving my car while eating a noodle bowl situated between my legs. Is that correct?"

"Yes, it's always funny even when you're saying it."

"And I'm steering the car with my thighs, right?"

"Yes. Yes!"

"That the thing is, Lauren, that wasn't me. You see, I pride myself on being a safe driver, a defensive driver. I would never text and drive let alone drive a car with my thighs while eating a noodle bowl. I fear that you're telling and retelling this story could cause me grave repercussions if ever my insurance agent catches wind of this yarn. Why, they could raise my insurance rates or cancel me altogether and send me to another less reputable agency. That would be most devastating. Also, though I am a fan of Asian food, I prefer to eat my meals at dining establishments or in the comfort of my own home. I do not wolf down food in my car, certainly not something as potentially messy as a noodle bowl. I'm thinking there's a possibility that this encounter on the road was all a dream to you, as old friends do pop up from time to time in dream imagery. It's also possible that this is merely a fantasy you've concocted, which is understandable as we are in the midst of the wedding season and emotions tend to be lighthearted and gay…"

"So, Lonny, you think it's a fantasy of mine to see you riding in your car with a noodle bowl between your legs and steering the car with you thighs?"

"Well, perhaps not a libidinous fantasy, but a fantasy to amuse yourself with nevertheless."

"But you do drive an older model green Honda?"

"Yes Lauren, but there are many of those on the road today."

"And you do wear those dorky glasses, and for some reason you wear your baseball cap backwards?"

"As do so many men my age…"

"That was you, motherfucker! You noodle bowl eating motherfucker!"

"Lauren, don't be crass."

"That was you eating that noodle bowl between your legs. That was you, Lonny. Just admit it."

"Now Lauren, I've stated my case plainly and sincerely and I want for you to cease and desist at once. Consider this matter case-closed."

"I thought you might say that, Lonny, since you were getting a bit testy at our last meeting. So I must tell you that when our cars came upon the street light I took some pictures."

"You took pictures of this?"

"And I blew them up."

"You blew them up? What are you, a psycho?"

"And I brought them here with me. Would you like to see them, Lonny? Close up?"

"Oh shit," he said, as she took the pictures from her purse and smoothed them out in front of him. "Listen, I was hungry. I was starving. I hadn't eaten all day. It was just one time. You must believe me, Lauren. You do believe me, don't you? How can we make this go away? Please, tell me how we can make this go away."

"Well," she said, "at all of these receptions not one person has asked me to dance. I think asking me to dance would be a good start."

It was a good start. One dance led to a second, and then a second to a third. Then there was the chicken dance and the hokey-pokey. After that a slow dance to end the evening. And then there were dates, there were promises, there was love, and then their own wedding. And the noodle bowl incident was never brought up again.

Rhymes with Spoon

The small town of Groverdale is known as the *'Poon Capital of the World.'* Here's how that happened: It was the Elderberry buddies who first noticed a dapper old man peering over a locked fence at the abandoned quarry. The Elderberries called it in to Sheriff Mann, telling him not to be alarmed, telling him that the old man did not appear to be up to any malfeasance. In fact, the old man bore a striking resemblance to Tom Harwood, the eccentric, extremely wealthy businessman from Ravenwood Meadows, the next town over. Could it be that Tom Harwood was scouting new locations for his next business venture? If the quarry were to be reopened, it would be a boon to nearly everyone in Groverdale; it would be a godsend for sure. Any way you slice it, this was big news.

Sheriff Mann raced to the quarry to try to intercept the old man, while at the same time putting a call of his own to the mayor, Beck Strother. Beck quickly summoned his three town council members while waiting for further updates from the sheriff. In due time all were gathered in the mayor's tiny office. There he held court. "Lady and gentlemen of the council, I am happy to report that a man fitting the description of Tom Harwood has been possibly spotted while scouting the quarry as a location for one of his new enterprises. This could be the opportunity we've been waiting for, our ticket back in. We'll be players again. It's fantastic news!"

"But did I hear you use the word *possibly*, Beck?" asked Councilman Doug Harvey. "Could you expound on that?"

"It was the Elderberry buddies who saw him down there," said the mayor, excitedly. "Now you know they've been right about many an issue before."

"It's true," said Councilman Earl Skullwinder. "Those boys were right about the tax lien of 2010."

"And they were right about correcting the flood plain," added Councilwoman Nancy Enright.

"But they were *wrong* about the steeple abutment," said Doug Harvey.

"Now, council, all of this is neither here nor there," said Mayor Strother. "If this boy isn't Tom Harwood we simply send him on his way. We lose nothing. But if it is Tom Harwood, and if Tom Harwood has intentions of reopening our quarry, then we give Tom Harwood whatever he wants. I don't care if it's blackberry flapjacks or turnips on toast. Whatever he wants he gets, right?"

"I just don't want to be bitten on the bottom by this," said the ever skeptical Doug Harvey.

"But Doug," said Nancy Enright, "if that quarry reopens we're golden, we're all the way back and then some. Let's just believe that those Elderberry buddies are right about this one. Let's say we just believe."

A call from Sheriff Mann ended their discussion. The mayor said into his phone, "Have you made contact?" He then put the sheriff on speakerphone so that everyone could participate.

"I have made contact," said Sheriff Mann. "I have him in the back of the car as a matter of fact. He sure is an agreeable little fellow."

"But is he Harwood?" interjected Doug Harvey. "That's the key issue here."

"Not so fast on that one," said Sheriff Mann. "Our old boy is a little confused, what with all the excitement. But if this man is not Tom Harwood, I would tell you that Tom Harwood has a twin brother. Does anyone know if Tom Harwood has a twin brother?"

"Look, we'll figure all that out later," said Mayor Strother. "Just ask him what he wants. We'll give him whatever he wants and sort out all that other stuff later. I heard over in Full Forks he wanted jelly jam from a rubberneck root and they gave it to him. Six months later there's a new factory in Full Forks. You see how this works."

"Well," said the sheriff, "he has been quite adamant about what he wants. Quite specific actually."

"Do tell, sheriff," said the mayor, "do tell. What's the matter, cat got your tongue?"

"Is the councilwoman there?" the sheriff questioned.

"Of course," the mayor replied. "We're all here."

"See, I don't like to speak French in front of the ladies," Sheriff Mann responded.

"Don't you worry about her," said Councilman Earl Skullwinder. "She's been around the block a time or two."

"Hey, I'm a divorcee," protested Councilwoman Nancy Enright. "That doesn't mean I've been *around the block*."

"Well, halfway around anyway," Earl muttered.

"Bite your tongue," shot back Nancy.

The mayor squelched their bickering with an abrupt hand gesture and returned his attention to the sheriff. "Just tell us what he wants, sheriff. I'll cover Nancy's ears if the talk gets too blue."

"All right, Beck, I'll tell you what he wants exactly as he put it to me. He said, and I quote, '*Skidilly-didilly-doodilly*, and all I want is poon.' I asked him to please repeat his request and he says to me, '*Fi-fiddily-fi-o*, and all I want is poon.'"

"Poon?" questioned an exasperated Mayor Strother. "Does that mean what I think it means? Poon?"

"I think it's pretty clear what he wants, Mr. Mayor," said the sheriff. "I reckon I've seen these poon hounds before once or twice. They don't stop just because they're in their twilight years. If anything, they charge harder. No time left on the clock and all that."

The mayor and the sheriff concluded their phone call after the sheriff promised he'd deliver the old man to the mayor's office in short order. Then the mayor looked upon his council. "Well, there are some things we can do about this."

"And there are some things we can't," cautioned Doug Harvey.

"Now Douglass," said the mayor, "don't get all prim and proper on us. Sometimes you've got to get dirty before you come clean."

"But Mr. Mayor?" said Doug Harvey.

"Now all of you," the mayor continued, "you remember that girl at the county fair, the one who ran the kissing booth? What's her name, Renee Houndstooth? Why I bet she'd be an eager beaver for such an assignment."

"But if you recall, Mr. Mayor," said Nancy Enright, "she only wanted to kiss the girls."

"Renee Houndstooth? Well I'll be damned."

"It's seems we have a shortage of eligible women in this town," said Earl Skullwinder. "That's a shame for all of us."

"But what about that girl," exclaimed the mayor, "that one just graduated from high school! What was on that t-shirt she used to wear? *No drugs, no thugs, just hugs* or something other than that. Well, this won't be much more than hugging, not with a man so old as Tom Harwood."

"Beck, please?" said Doug Harvey. "Can't we just buy him a backscratcher or a cheese plate?"

"Besides," said Nancy Enright, "her latest t-shirt says something like *'You ain't getting a thing until I see that ring!'*"

"I guess she's just the marrying type," said the mayor, sadly. "I guess there are all kinds and types."

"Well," said Earl Skullwinder, "I hate to call out the elephant in the room…"

"Earl Skullwinder, I will kill you," said Nancy.

"Now Nancy," said Earl, "you're always going on about how we need to be team players, how we need to sacrifice for the welfare of the team. I believe myself and the other gentlemen in this room would do what needs to be done only we don't have the requisite parts for the operation. You understand?"

"You want me to be a whore, a quarry whore!"

"Oh Nancy, that's foul," said the mayor. "We want no such thing. It's just that, well, you're our last hope. So you take him out for drinks, you dance him around the floor, maybe a peck on the cheek. It doesn't necessarily need to come to its fruition. Maybe he passes out early? You know how these geezers roll."

Sheriff Mann rolled up and escorted the old man to the mayor's office. After a brief exchange of pleasantries Mayor Strother said to the old man, "Please tell, sir, are you man called Tom Harwood from Ravenwood Meadows?"

"Ravenwood Meadows you say?" said the old man. "I can tell you I've been to and from so many different places."

"But you're Tom?" said the mayor.

"Tom," repeated the old man just above a whisper.

This was good enough for the mayor for he nudged Nancy forward in the face of the old man. She towered over him. "Well Tom, here she is. Do you like her?"

"Oh, very much so," said the old man. "I like her very much indeed."

Nancy took the old man by the arm and escorted him out of the office. The others had their own opinions. "Well that cinches it for me," said Councilman Earl Skullwinder. "That guy looks just like Tom Harwood. It has to be him. He's a carbon copy for what I know."

"I'm not so sure," replied Councilman Doug Harvey. "He could be anyone, a simple drifter maybe."

"Well, if a factory drifts on in here I'm all for that," said the mayor. "For the simple price of poon? Are you kidding me?"

It was three hours later and Nancy Enright staggered back into the office, her cheeks reddened and her breathing heavy. All were gathered and cocktails shared among them. They rose from their seats immediately. "Nancy, are you all right?" inquired Mayor Strother. "Did he hurt you?"

"Oh no," said Nancy, "not hurt at all but certainly winded and worn out. One of you better pour me a drink real fast."

"Tell us, Nancy," said Doug Harvey. "Tell us what he wants, or if he's gotten all he wanted and we can now have ours."

"Well," said Nancy, "I gave him all I could and the minutes turned into hours. That little tumbleweed has no off-button from all I could tell. When he finally did come up for air, do you know what he had the nerve to say to me?"

"Do tell, Nancy," said Earl Skullwinder. "Please."

"He said, *Ti–tick–tickory, and all I want is poon.*'"

"More poon!" exclaimed the mayor. "Why that man is insatiable."

"I'm sorry you did all that for nothing," said Doug Harvey.

"Nothing?" said Nancy. "Are you kidding me? If that was nothing then I'll have a helping of nothing every day. That old rascal still has some pepper in his pot."

"Well, we'll just have to get him more poon then," said Mayor Strother.

"Funny, but I don't think it's that," said Nancy. "I mean, he's saying one thing but perhaps thinking another."

"Whatever do you mean, Nancy?" asked Doug Harvey.

"I mean perhaps it's some sort of riddle," Nancy continued. "It could be that we're to solve the riddle and then get the factory we so desire."

"I have no time for riddles," said councilman Earl Skullwinder. "I say we put him in a cell with Crazy Pete. If anyone can get it out of him, it's Crazy Pete."

"No," said Nancy, "I don't want to see him hurt."

"Crazy Pete may be crazy," said the mayor, "but he wouldn't hurt a fly. He rents a cell in the jail because he doesn't want to go home to his wife. Have you met his wife? He was known as Turkey leg Pete before she got hold of him."

"I remember old Turkey leg," one of them chimed in.

They soon came to the conclusion that having the old man share a cell with Crazy Pete wasn't such a bad idea. Mayor Strother had Sheriff Mann brief Crazy Pete on the situation, and after long escorted the old man to the prison cell. They told the old man they were holding him for some sort of trespassing violation. He didn't seem to mind being detained. In fact, he seemed quite pleased, him being an agreeable sort of fellow.

The sheriff made a brief introduction, "Crazy Pete, old man. Old man, Crazy Pete," before slamming the cell door. Then they were alone. Crazy Pete spoke first. "So I hear you're a poon man."

"Yes, I quite like it," said the old man.

"Blondes, brunettes, redheads?"

"Yes."

"Look," said Crazy Pete, "I want to know what you want with these nice people, but I don't want to hear any of this fiddly-faddily-foodily stuff that I hear you been dishing out. Now you tell me what it is you want, and I'll decide whether or not to bash your head in."

"I want poon!"

"You've had your poon, old man. Now I'm getting my hammer. Maybe you'll speak with more clarity after I lump you one."

"You see, they taste so good," said the old man.

"The women?"

"Yes, the women," the old man continued, "but also the nuts."

"Nuts? What nuts?" questioned Crazy Pete.

"Poon nuts of course. They drop from the leaves of the Finicula tree this time of year."

"Finicula tree? Why you daffy old man!"

"Yes," continued the old man. "Poon nuts. For I have searched so long, so far, over hill and dale for just one Finicula tree. And here I find it just beyond the fence in your quarry. So close and yet so far I'm afraid."

"So all you want is some nuts?"

"Not some," said the old man. "I want many, perhaps a whole bag. I'll gladly pay my share and even then some. They're quite tasty, and also good for one's digestion."

"Good grief," said Crazy Pete. "Nuts."

Later on, they gave the old man his one bag of poon nuts because that's all he would accept. After that he went on his way, skipping free and merry down the twisted, wooded trail. They never did find out if he was really the rich Tom Harwood of Ravenwood Meadows, but it really didn't matter. For the quarry was no longer a quarry or a potential factory of any kind. It was now a tree farm, a Finicula tree farm that would drop a plethora of poon nuts each season and make the small town of Groverdale the *'Poon Capital of the World.'* That's how that happened.

The Gift of Giving

Richard brought in the mail and met his wife, Ginger, in the kitchen. "Anything good?" she asked.

"Looks like something from Barry," Richard mumbled.

"Barry? Why would he send you anything?"

"Let's find out," said Richard as he tore at the envelope.

Richard held up the simple, flowery 'thank you' note for Ginger to see. "How nice, and so unexpected from Barry," she said. "He's never seemed the type to offer a card."

Richard's face grew red. Something was wrong. "This is no ordinary thank you note, Ginger. He's mocking me."

"Mocking you? Richard, please. Whatever do you mean?"

"The note reads: *Richard, thank you so much for the ball-scratcher you gave me for my birthday. I really needed one and it works just fine. Regards, Barry.*"

"Well that's just lovely sentiment," said Ginger.

"I did not give him a ball-scratcher!" snapped Richard.

"I'm afraid I don't understand."

"It was an artifact. What I gave him was an ancient artifact. You hang it in your kitchen. You certainly don't scratch your balls with it. You see the way he sticks it to me? You see what he's doing, don't you?"

"Was that the artifact you bartered for while you were ankle deep in desert sands?" Ginger asked.

"No, no, no. I did barter for sure, bartered with my life as a matter of fact. But I wasn't in the desert, I was knee deep in Amazonian mud for this one. How can he be so ungrateful?"

"Maybe it's just a misunderstanding," said Ginger, "because it looks…"

"I don't care what it looks like," said Richard. "It was an artifact, and it's ancient, and it's supposed to hang in the kitchen. Why can't he see that and appreciate what I've done for him, this precious gift I've given him, nearly costing me my own life in the process?"

"Oh, dear Richard," Ginger soothed. "My poor, dear, Richard. You must talk to Barry. Tell him how it hurts you when he writes such boorish things, so common, so sophomoric. It's beneath him."

Ginger held Richard's drooped head until he was over his petulance. Richard then gathered himself and went into his den. He called Barry. "We need to talk, Barry. Now."

They met on a park bench somewhere in the neighborhood between their homes. Children played in the distance and clouds wafted above the warm sky. It was a perfect summer evening. "So what did you drag me out here for, Richard?"

"I think you know, Barry."

"No, I'm afraid I don't know."

"You insulted my wife," said Richard.

"What? Are you crazy? I love Ginger. I would never insult Ginger."

"She happened to be with me when I opened your *so-called* thank you note. She saw the way you insulted my gift by referring to it as a *ball-scratcher*. We were both deeply offended."

"It's not a ball-scratcher, Richard? Then what the hell is it?"

"It's an ancient artifact. I told you that when I gave it to you at your birthday party."

"I thought you were kidding."

"Barry, I risked my life for that artifact. I could have been killed."

"Are you sure you want to go with that story, Richard? You risked your life? Think hard, my friend, think hard…"

"Of course I do. Of course, Barry. I was in the Amazon. I was knee deep in the muck and I did this for you, for my friend of forty years. I did this for you, Barry."

"Well, you shouldn't have," stated Barry. "You really shouldn't have."

"But I did. Yes Barry, I did. And now let us recall the gift you gave me for my birthday. It was a stainless steel beer stein, fair enough. But please note the inscription: *To my friend, Richard, the biggest Dick I know.* That is what you wrote to me. How dare you!"

"But that's funny. I was just trying to be funny."

"Okay, mister funny man, let me tell you something: I happen to have a glass cabinet where I keep all my memorable gifts. It's a locked cabinet, Barry. It's locked. Perhaps you've seen it?"

"Oh, I've seen it, Richard, and it's my ultimate fantasy to break into your house and pick that diary lock you've got on that stupid cabinet. I'll show you."

"Well, let me tell you something, Barry, your funny beer stein did not make the glass cabinet. No, sir."

"Oh my God, Richard, I'm mortally wounded by this slight."

"I'll tell you where your gift resides, Barry. Oh, I'll tell you all right. It sits on my desk holding pens and pencils I will no doubt ever use. That's all it's good for, joker. It will never see a drop of beer or the glass cabinet for that matter. Never ever."

"Oh, la-di-da. But let me tell you about a gift I received from you, Richard, just five short years ago."

"Don't you go there, Barry."

"I will go there, Richard, I will. At my birthday party as you well recall, in front of everybody, I open a gift from you that's a vibrator, a sexual device."

"It was not intended as a sexual device, Barry. You'd been complaining about your neck. You remember your neck pain? It was a neck massager what I bought for you. I was looking out for my friend."

"I'm afraid neck massagers aren't shaped like nine inch phalluses. I don't suppose you'd put something like that in your precious glass cabinet."

"Look, let's cool this down a bit," said Richard. "We've been friends forty years, right? I'll say I overreacted, okay?"

"Okay, Richard, okay. But one more thing before we go. I'm not sure if you inspected your little artifact as closely as I did. But if you turn it over and look at the bottom it clearly reads: *Made in China*. So I'm not exactly sure how it got to your Amazon jungle."

"The Chinese can do anything these days."

"Also, I know it looks like wood, but it's definitely plastic, your artifact. I'm guessing you were put out what, five bucks for it?"

"I can prove it, Barry. We can take it down to the university lab right now. That artifact is genuine. It should be hanging in your kitchen."

"I know we can go down to the university, Richard. I know we can. But we've gone down this road before and it always leads to your embarrassment. Always. You sure you want to go through with it?"

Richard thought hard about it but then abruptly rose from his seat. "No. No, I guess I give in. Looks like you got me, Barry. You got me. You win. I'll go home now."

Richard started walking away but Barry caught up to him. "Richard, wait up. Wait up. I just want to say one more thing."

"Go ahead," he replied sheepishly. "Give me whatever I deserve."

"No," said Barry, "let me get this out. I just want to sincerely thank you for the gift I received from you. I'm real sorry I insulted it, whatever it is, and I'll find a real nice place to hang it."

"No, it's okay," Richard shrugged. "It's just a cheap trinket. Probably really is a ball-scratcher."

"Look, we're friends forty years, Richard, and I'm not about to let you go. And hey, maybe some day I'll get something into that glass cabinet of yours. You'll see."

"You just might," said Richard with a wave. "My friend, you just might."

Meat and Cheese

Tommy Cornwall was with both of his parents as the three confidently strode up the steps to the testing center. On this day Tommy would learn if he was being accepted into the *Gifted Program*, where all his classes would be now be advanced placement, and he'd have a clear road to the Ivy League and beyond. "Nothing can stop me now," said Tommy at the top of the steps. "Right, Pop?"

Tommy's father gave his son a stern look of caution but said nothing. He certainly didn't want to jinx anything, not after they'd come so far. Mr. Cornwall held his wife tightly to him while being led down the hall by Tommy to the testing center's entrance. Once inside the reception area they noticed some other kids and families milling about. They'd have to wait their turn.

Finally the Cornwall name was called out by the weary receptionist and they bounded into an interior office. A panel of three greeted them from behind a large table, then everyone took a seat. A tall, thin, pointy man in a white lab coat spoke first. "Thank you for coming in today," he said in a cheerful voice. "I must say yours is a most interesting case."

"Interesting," said Tommy's father. "How so?"

"Well," the pointy man said, "usually our results are quantified. If you scored, say, a 95 or above we would likely consider you gifted academically."

"So how'd I do?" said Tommy. "What was my score?"

"That's just it," said pointy, "there was no score."

"No score?" questioned Tommy. "What gives?"

"That isn't to say you scored zero," continued pointy. "It's just that for some reason the computer refused to tabulate a score for you, simply refused. It's most unusual, unheard of really. It left us all scratching our heads."

"Well," said Tommy's mother, "does this mean my little boy is gifted or not?"

Now the female of the white lab coats spoke up. "Since there was no score for the young applicant, we had to rely on his interviews with our staff. There were some key words that came out during these interviews that, quite frankly, caused concern for our evaluation."

"Key words?" said Tommy. "What kind of key words are we talking about here?"

"One word that popped up time and time again was, well, *nudnik*," said lab coat lady. "As in, 'Who is this nudnik that thinks he's gifted?'"

"Nudnik," said Tommy. "I'm a nudnik?"

"This is appalling," spoke Tommy's father. "Do you know this young man is the inventor of the Alternator/Regulator? When it's not alternating it's regulating…"

"And when it's not regulating it's alternating," added Tommy's mother.

"Look," said the last of the lab coats, a portly man with bad pants, "kids are always inventing this or that. It just doesn't factor in with what we're trying to evaluate. And the 'nudnik' comment wasn't isolated by any means. Other comments referred to the young applicant as a *doofus*, a *gomer*, a *rube*, a *blockhead*, a *nimrod*, a *nincompoop*, a *dullard*, a *numbskull*, a *simpleton*, a *dunderhead*, a *dolt*, a *drip*, a *dim bulb* and a *dunce*. Why, one interviewer said he didn't think the young man had any actual brains per say, but just a spacious cavity filled with meat and cheese."

"Say, that's a lot to be piling up on a guy," said Tommy. "And since when does he get to crack wise with that meat and cheese stuff?"

"But there is a silver lining here," pointy lab coat chimed in. "Although we cannot accept your boy into our gifted program, we have lined up a job opportunity for him, something more on his level."

"A job opportunity?" said Tommy. "Can you beat that, Pops?"

"Well I for one am insulted," said Tommy's pop, "and I'm not even the one they were insulting."

"Wait a minute," said Tommy. "I want to hear more about this job opportunity. If you says I'm a nudnik, I want to make sure it pays."

"The job is at Softey's Mattress Company," said pointy. "You would be the mattress tester, meaning all you would have to do is lie down on the mattress in the window display and look comfortable. With your abilities, young man, I think you could go quite far in the mattress testing industry."

"See that, Pop? There's always a silver lining. And Ma, you're always telling me I should get more sleep, right? I think this is great news all around. Let's get down to Softey's straight away."

"And if I may speak for the others," said lady lab coat, "we just want to thank you, Mr. Cornball, for coming in today. I know some of this was rather difficult to hear."

"Wait just a minute here," said Tommy. "Did you say *Cornball*? I'm not Cornball, I'm Cornwall."

"So you're not *Lenny Cornball*?" asked pointy.

"No, I'm Tommy Cornwall through and through."

"I'm his mother and I say he's Tommy Cornwall. His nickname is Scooty if you must know."

"Oh my," said pointy. "I'm afraid we've made a terrible mistake. Please, somebody bring up Tommy's score."

"Tommy Cornwall scored…99," said portly, aghast. "He is gifted. By every indication this boy is indeed gifted."

"That's my Tommy!" shouted Tommy's pop, leaping from his seat. "What other boy his age would invent an Alternator/Regulator?"

"And we do want to get a look at that invention of yours, Mr. Cornwall. We'll put our best people at your disposal."

"Well," said Tommy, "I can't say I'm surprised. I knew there was much more than meat and cheese inside this old noodle brain."

"Welcome to the gifted program, Tommy," said pointy. "But it sure looks like we've got some bad news for Lenny."

Men Against Onions!

(And women too, but we can't find any to support our cause.)

We stand before you today to tell you the truth, that onions do not complement your food, that they do in fact ruin many a fine meal. Sure, they are aromatic as fried rings or with steak fajitas, but that's as far as we'll go — and the good smells are the devil's trickery I may add. Don't be fooled. There are now farmers (or should I call them what they rightly are — pushers!) in Videlia, Georgia who live high on the hog by bringing this vile food source to market. And who asked for these onions? Certainly not us. But they are thrust upon us and how can this be? I recently ordered a hamburger which did not advertise having any onions. But lo and behold what sits upon this hamburger but a giant, greasy onion. Certainly I offered complaint, and was rebuffed at once with "I thought everybody liked onions." Oh no, madam, everybody does not. We can't get away from these things. We're inundated; it's impossible to eat out. Just move them to side people say, brushing our anti-onion concerns off with laughs all around. But I say, would you do that with a rat? Would you just move it to the side and continue your fine dining?

I admit to being fooled when my friend, Edward R., told me that onions were first discovered in the 1850's by a naturalist by the name of Willard O'Dawson. Good one, Edward R., real funny. But further research indicates that the evil ones have been around for over 7000 years. Ancient Egyptians may have even worshipped onions. Worship? Can you beat that? In the middle ages onions were given as gifts and even used as currency. If anybody tries buy something with an onion from me, I will tell them this: Your money is no good here, sir! Additional research indicates that doctors prescribed onions to facilitate bowel movements, aid in erections, and even promote hair growth. If I ever need an onion to get me going in the sack, that will most certainly be a dark day for this Romeo. Upon study, I will concede that onions contain something called flavonoids and phenolics that have the potential to be anti-inflammatory, anti-cancer, and anti-oxidant (and anti-taste I might add). It almost sounds as if I'm promoting this vile weed but surely I am not. *Men Against Onions* will use every opportunity to speak out against Big O and its minions. There are two of us now, but we will certainly grow exponentially now that you have heard our declaration. Onions beware, *Men Against Onions* is upon you. BROTHERS, UNITE AS ONE AND COME FORTH! Brothers? Anybody? Is this microphone even on? All right, I'll go…

It's Just a Service I Provide

For as long as he could remember, Les Archer had always gone door to door. He'd shoveled snow in winter, mowed lawns in summer, had early morning newspaper routes, sold Fuller brushes, vacuum cleaners, encyclopedias, and magazine subscriptions. He been chased by angry dogs, chased by even angrier husbands, and been unceremoniously removed from properties by security guards. And now what? Les was a tried and true door to door man, but now there was less to go door to door about. Les was dejected. Had he nothing left to offer in this world? He took a good look in the mirror and used his old trick to regain his confidence. *"Les is more,"* he said to himself. "Les is more, Les is more, Les is more, LES IS MORE!" Composure restored, he headed back onto the street, back to what he knew best, back to door to door.

The first door he hit nobody was home, or pretended they weren't home. The second door was dark and spooky so he passed on this one. The third was promising. A cottage home with a picket fence and a nice pelt of green grass. Les tipped up his fedora and knocked upon the door. Eventually a man answered. He was tall and wore glasses. His sweater was light gray. "Hello," the man said. "What can I do for you?"

"No, sir. It's what I can do for you. My name is Les Archer," he said, extending his hand to the tall man in the gray sweater. "And I would like to provide you a service."

"A service, huh. And what kind of service would that be?"

"But sir, first I would like to ask if there's a lady of the house present?"

"Sally's home. She certainly is."

"That's wonderful, sir," said Les. "You see, in my experience, there are services some husbands extend to their wives enthusiastically, some do so grudgingly, while some do so not at all."

"And what kind of services are you referring to, Mr. Archer?"

"Why I'm referring to the ancient practice of the foot rub. And you know, this is not a sexual activity. Heavens no. This is merely therapeutic, just a service I provide. Are you a husband who provides such an undertaking, or would you rather outsource to a professional?"

"Well, normally I'm a husband who regularly engages in this activity, but of late I did bang my thumb on the copy machine at work. So providing such a service myself would put me in a great deal of pain."

"I am so sorry to hear of your injury," said Les, "but I am pleased that my timing appears to be exact."

"It's like you knew," said the man.

"Indeed it is."

The tall man in the gray sweater called out to his wife, who was apparently upstairs. "Oh Sally, there's a stranger at the door. He'd like to rub your feet."

"Rub my feet?" answered Sally. "Say, I wasn't born yesterday."

"No, Sally," said the tall man. "It's nothing untoward. It's a foot massage, something therapeutic, a professional service he would provide."

"A foot rub, huh? That doesn't sound so bad. What's he charge? I don't want to be a chump."

"Ten dollars a foot," Les called up to her. "No more, no less. Everyday low prices are what I gladly offer."

"Ten dollars a foot?" said Sally. "That's a bargain where I come from. Send him on up, Mel. With those prices, I'll have both feet done for sure."

"Swell," said Les, bounding up the stairs.

Les talked to Sally as he rubbed her feet with lotion. He told her which pressure points on the heel aided digestion, which stimulated the mind, and which, right along the arch, had a direct connection to the…

"Ohhhhhhhhh," Sally moaned. "You really hit the spot that time. You do that again and I'm going to be singing opera."

Twenty minutes later Sally called down to her husband. "Honey, guess what? Mr. Archer is offering fifty percent off a bikini wax for today only. Fifty percent off? Can you beat that?"

"Fifty percent off?" said Mel. "Hot dog!"

Les Archer was back in business, big time. Les is more, baby. Les is more!

Highwaters

(and other love songs)

Security guard and songwriter Tommy Feely walked into the reception area of the office of Mr. Wallace Strong, head of music publishing at Wonderdog Records. The office was immense, and crowded with other hopefuls such as Tommy. He introduced himself to the receptionist.

"Oh," she said. "So you're Mr. Feely. Please, go right in. Mr. Strong is expecting you."

"Really?" questioned Tommy. "Go right in? Me?"

"Of course," she replied, gesturing toward the large door with Mr. Strong's name on it. "Go right in."

The other folks in the reception area glared at Tommy, but what could he do? His heart was madly beating but enter the door he did. A large man smoking a cigar sat behind the biggest desk he'd ever seen. Tommy crossed deep shag carpeting and made his way toward the desk. "Ah, Mr. Feely," said Wallace Strong. "So good of you to come."

"I can't believe I got in to see so soon, Mr. Strong. It's such an honor to meet you."

Tommy reached his right hand as far as he could across the vast desk, and was just able enough to shake hands with Wallace Strong. After further pleasantries Tommy was offered a chair. He could barely see over and across the desk but at least he was in *his* office, the great Wally Strong of Wonderdog Records.

"Tommy, I'm a blunt man. Do you mind that I'm a blunt man?"

"No, Mr. Strong, not at all. In fact I kind of prefer it."

"That's swell, Tommy, swell," said Mr. Strong. "Now before we get started we have to do something about you name. Tommy Feely does nothing for me, understand? It's nothing against you, but I don't see you as a Tommy, I see you as a Touchy."

"*Touchy Feely?*"

"Exactly. Touchy Feely. Now that is a name to remember. One day, Touchy Feely will see his name up in lights."

"Well," said Tommy (or Touchy), "I guess that's okay."

"Great, kid, now show me what you've got. Knock my socks off."

Touchy forked over the sheets to his first song and let Mr. Strong peruse at his leisure. "So, you're song is called…"

"Highwaters. That's right, Mr. Strong."

"And it's about pants?"

"That's correct."

"Let me read back to you the lyrics so that we're on the same page. That okay with you, Touchy?"

"Certainly, Mr. Strong."

"Highwaters!

Did your mama buy those pants?

Highwaters!

Don't even think that you can dance.

Highwaters!

Kid, you never had a chance.

Highwaters!

Are you preparing for a flood?

Highwaters!

You got protection from the mud.

Highwaters!

How you gonna ever score some bud?"

Wallace Strong stared at the sheet for a long time. Touchy fidgeted in his seat. Finally Mr. Strong lowered the sheet. "Is there a melody to this, some music to go with the words?"

"Not quite yet, though there will definitely be music. Most definitely."

"You know what, kid?" said Mr. Strong. "Forget about the music. We'll add the music later, any kind of music will do. Listen, Touchy, what you've given me here is pure gold, solid gold with a bullet to the top. It's dynamite. Man, where did you get this?"

"I'm so glad you like it, Mr. Strong. I thought I had something and now you've confirmed it. I'm so overjoyed."

"Kid, Wally Strong has been in the business for a log time and I know a winner when I see one. You've got moxie, you've got the chops. Kid, do you know who is on the Mount Rushmore of songwriters?"

"I have no idea."

"There's Bob Dylan, Lennon & McCartney…and you."

"Me?"

"Kid," said Mr. Wallace Strong, "with just one song you've pushed Joni Mitchell off of Mount Rushmore. What do you think of that?"

"I love Joni Mitchell."

"Kid!" shouted Mr. Strong. "Touchy Feely takes a back seat to nobody — not even Joni Mitchell. You hear?"

"Yes, sir."

Wally Strong immediately picked up his phone. Before dialing he said to Touchy, "Listen, I've got an in with Katy Perry's people. Watch me work."

Mr. Strong spoke with a Rodney on the other end of the line. He informed Rodney that there was a new player in the game, one Touchy Feely, and Katy Perry better get on board or his songs go straight to Miley. Rodney let him know that Katy would record his song tomorrow. That wasn't good enough for Wally Strong. "If you want a Touch Feely song, Rodney, you record today! None of this tomorrow shit."

So Katy Perry soon released *Highwaters* and, of course, it went straight to the top. Now they wanted more gold from Touchy Feely.

"Kid," said Wally Strong, "what have you got for me?"

"It's a song I call *Smitty Did It*. Mostly instrumental but in the background every once in a while you hear the words 'Smitty did it.' I haven't got the music yet, but…"

"Smitty did it? What'd he do?"

"Hell if I know."

"Kid, just when I think you can't possibly top yourself, you top yourself. It's unbelievable. Because, as we all know, kids are crazy about jazz!"

I Could Do You

Rick had been fired that afternoon. His desk cleaned out, there was nothing left to do but leave the office, for good. Last box in hand he headed for the door. But wait, there was one last stop: Cindy's desk. But more importantly, Cindy herself behind Cindy's desk. Rick was in the unique position of really having nothing left to lose. He could speak his mind. He had something important to say. He said to Cindy, "I could do you."

"*You could do me?*" questioned Cindy. "That's preposterous. You could never do me."

"I could so do you," said Rick, "and everyone knows it. The security guard knows it, the lunch lady knows it, the kid in the mail room knows it, even the big boss knows it. Everyone knows it. The question is, why don't you?"

"Because you only think you can do me. The people that *do me* know they can do me. You with your mail room boy, your security guard, and even your big boss. You're tiny men, you come up to my ankles, you're pesky piss ants. I'm afraid you could never do me. No, it's unthinkable."

"I could do you and then you would be done," said Rick. "Do you understand me? What I'm saying is, no other men after me would interest you in the slightest. I think you're afraid of that."

"Afraid?" laughed Cindy. "I think not. Like I said, you only think you can do me. I catch trepidation from men rather easily. You shuffle your feet, lose eye contact, stammer a little. Sorry, but you melt in my presence. I'd eat you alive."

"You talk tough, sister, but I see right through your act. I've seen the way you check me out, I caught you looking at my ass. I stand by what I said. Simply put, Cindy, I could do you."

"When?" she asked.

"*When?*"

That's right, stud, you heard me. When can do me?"

Rick thought about it for a second — maybe too long a second. "Tonight," he finally said. "I can do you tonight."

"No," said Cindy. "I can't wait that long. I want you to do me right now."

"Right now?" questioned Rick. "Are you crazy?"

"It's not crazy at all. I want you to do me right now, right here. What are they going to do, fire you again? I'm the one taking the chances here."

"Look," said Rick, "I'm a classy guy. I like clean sheets, I like music and candlelight. I'm not doing it in an office."

"You're pathetic."

"What's wrong with tonight? It's just a couple hours…"

"You creeps are all the same. You disgust me."

"Listen," said Rick, "let's just get the facts straight before I leave the office. It's been officially determined that I could do you. It's official and there's nothing you can do about it."

"Yes, it's been officially determined that you *could* have done me," said Cindy, a wicked smile creeping across her face. "But you didn't — and you never will."

You're the Top!

Bottoms usually ate a late lunch in the break room at the office. He was more than likely alone then, and he liked it that way. He read his newspaper in peace while enjoying a sandwich, a soda, and maybe some chips. The break room consisted of four tables and a scattering of chairs. There was nothing on the walls except a poster explaining the minimum wage and a guide to the Heimlich maneuver. There was one machine that dispensed sodas and another that dispensed chips and other snacks. Bottoms sat furthest from the snack and soda machines because the soda one made a humming sound that irritated his ears. This was the break room on that day, quiet, sparse, and horribly dull until another employee entered the room.

Bottoms lowered his newspaper enough to regard the man that came into the room. He knew him, vaguely, as one of the newer employees on the staff. The man did not seem to notice Bottoms at all. He made right for the soda machine and tossed in some money. When his soda popped out he exclaimed "Yes!" Now he was throwing money down the snack machine. This time he was not so lucky. The chips fell only halfway down the front of the glass-encased machine before getting caught up on something that prevented its fall. The chips were quite stuck, and the man appeared helpless to intercede. "Oh no," he cried. "Oh no. What's happened here?"

The man placed his soda on the nearest table. He said aloud, "Now don't you go anywhere," presumably speaking to the soda itself. But he did not regard Bottoms at all, and now Bottoms was watching the man with keen curiosity. The man returned to the machine and got down on his knees. He made a feeble attempt to reach under the machine in order to somehow free the chips manually. But his arm was too small and surely the machine had safeguards against such a procedure. In good time he withdrew his arm and resumed an upright position. Now he grasped the machine as if to hug it, and them began violently shaking it until the floor rumbled. He ceased the shaking motion when he could see that his efforts were of no use. The chips weren't going anywhere.

The man put his hands on his hips. "Now you tell me what's going on here," he said to the machine, his back to Bottoms. "You tell me what's going on here. We had a deal, a contract if you will. I give you money, you give me chips. I *gave* you money…and now what's this? You *claim* a technical difficulty and that's that? I have no recourse. Is that it? Well, I'm afraid it's not going to be that simple. You see, I'd hardly had any breakfast this morning and now I'm *so* hungry. I'm office hungry, you know, the kind where you'd lick the paint off the walls, the kind where'd you'd eat old Halloween candy, the kind where you'd steal another's lunch from the refrigerator. I've been thinking of having chips and a soda all day long and I was so looking forward to your kind services. I had the money. *You know I had the money!* And now what do you do? You dangle these chips right before my very eyes. You tease me with this supposed malfunction. Sir, I am not a violent man by any means, but look what you've done to me? I must raise my fists to you, you gnarly scalawag. I must attack and attack I will!"

Bottoms was now in a strange, unenviable position. He could have mad a quick exit from the room and notify the proper authorities. He could have interceded and made an attempt to help this man dislodge his chips in lieu of violence. But, as happens in human nature, sometimes one does nothing at all. This is what Bottoms did as the man bent his knees, clenched his fists, and growled cat-like at the machine. Suddenly he jabbed with his right arm and struck the machine with a loud bang. But, alas, the machine was unfazed. "Ouch. That smarts," the man said, cupping his injured paw. Next, he kicked the machine hard but this did nothing. He kicked again and nothing still. "Gee whiz," he said, dejected. "You're one tough cookie."

Now the man strode all the way across the room from the machine, near to Bottoms but still apparently not noticing his presence. "So this is what it's come down to," said the man. "I'm going to take a running start and ram my head into your glass. No, I don't want to do this, but this is the course that you've chosen. You deny me my chips, I deny you your precious glass. You may be a match for my body, but you are no match for my heart. I declare on this day that I will have my chips. As God is my witness, thy chips shall be free!"

"Wait!" cried Bottoms, grabbing the back the man's shirt to prevent his suicidal charge.

"What's this?" asked the man, startled. "Unhand me, sir!"

"Wait. Just hear me out," said Bottoms. "Your name is Sparky, right?"

"Sparky?" questioned the man. "What am I, a dog? Sir, my name is Smedley."

"Oh, sorry," said Bottoms. "But Smedley, really, I think there's another way."

"Another way? How so?"

"Yes," said Bottoms. "You see, just moments before you entered the room, I myself purchased a bag of chips. But here now, it's the strangest thing. Rather than getting one bag of chips, the machine granted me two. In my possession I have two bags of chips."

"Two bags for one?" said Smedley. "Bonus! It's as if you'd won the lottery."

"Of course it would be indulgent of me to consume two bags of chips in one sitting, so won't you have the other, Smedley?"

"You want to give me a free bag of chips, just like that? Hey, what's the catch? What gives?"

"No catch at all, Smedley. Please, I just want to offer you a bag."

"Say, what's you name?"

"I'm Bottoms."

"Well, Bottoms, I say you're the tops — if you don't mind a little humor there."

"No I don't, Mr. Smedley. I don't mind at all."

So, each with a bag of chips, there in the break room was the start of a long and beautiful friendship.

In a Little Bookshop
at the Train Station…

In the city of Denver there is a little bookshop at the train station. It hasn't been there for long, or maybe, somehow, it has…

It was getting late, and getting cold outside, and Romero had but one customer in his bookshop. He could take it easy, he could reflect. Romero looked around his shop with pride. There were chocolates and candy and mints for sale, and as well sodas, post cards, aspirins, tourist trinkets, t-shirts, newspapers, magazines, and, of course…books. It amazed Romero at just how many books you could stuff into such a tiny store. It amazed him more at the great number of them he'd read over the course of his life. So many books, he thought, who will be left to read them?

Romero eyed a young customer as he browsed the shelves. He was a young man, tall, and dressed very well for his age, for this part of town. This was a man who took his time, Romero considered, a thoughtful man. After he finished browsing the young man turned to Romero. "Do you mind if I sit?" he said, gesturing to one of the two stuffed chairs in the shop. "It's so noisy in the concourse and so quiet in here. I'm afraid my train has been delayed."

"Please, sit," said Romero. "It's nice to have someone who appreciates the quiet. Tell me, where will the train take you this evening?"

"I'm headed for Chicago," said the young man. "I have some business there, and then I'll pass through again next week on my way home to LA."

"Such a long journey," said Romero. "I wish you well."

Romero noticed that the young man did not pick a book from the shelves. His hands were empty. "Did you not find a book you'd like to read while on the train?"

"Oh, I'm sorry," said the young man. "I saw many that looked promising, but I do have book with me already, in my luggage. It's called *True Grit*, by Charles Portis. Have you read that one?"

"Of course I have," replied Romero. "It's wonderful. But you know, it's such an exciting book, with so much action and adventure, that I believe you will be finished with this book before you even get to Chicago. Better have two to be safe."

"But I'm a very slow reader and I want to give all my attention to True Grit. Besides, I'm not really sure what I want to read next."

Romero paused for a moment and then gave the young man a long look. "You're going to Chicago on business, correct?"

"Correct."

"But if you could go anywhere, not for business but for pleasure, where would you go?"

The young man stroked his bare chin while pondering Romero's question. "I've recently seen this movie, *Vicky Cristina Barcelona*, so I think I would like to go to Spain, to Barcelona. It looked so nice. I want to eat paella in Barcelona. That would be such fun."

"Of course it would!" said Romero. "And I will write down for you three places where you can eat paella in Barcelona. Don't go to the beach. You'll get tourist paella and that's no good. I want you to get real Barcelona paella!"

"Yes, that's what I want."

Romero slipped the young man the paper with his notes, then stepped back and put his hands on his hips. "Now, for the book you must read. I will go and get it."

Romero walked down to the very end of the fiction section and grabbed the last book on the shelf. He smiled as he held the book high over his head and then quickly returned to the young man. "I have in my hand *The Shadow of the Wind* by Carlos Ruiz Zafon. You must read this before you go to Barcelona. You must."

"Well, maybe I will if I must," said the young man. "What's it about?"

"It's about a boy in Barcelona whose father takes him to a mysterious mansion that is filled with endless aisles and tall shelves with nothing but books. The boy is allowed to take one book and one book only. This will be his book."

"Does he like it, his book?" asked the young man.

"Does he like it? Oh, you bet he likes it. He loves it. The book has magic and intrigue and danger and love. And it seems to come alive in a way when a murky man in the shadows comes to steal the boy's book away."

"But why should he do that?"

"You have to read the book — and then you must go to Barcelona."

"Well," said the young man, "perhaps you could hold it for me because I do have to make my train. I'll read True Grit on the way to Chicago, and then on my way back to LA I'll stop in and get this one."

"Boy, you're a tough sale," sighed Romero. "Okay, I will hold it for you. Tell me your name."

"Semper. That's my last name. I'm Dan."

"I am Romero, and I will hold this book for you until you return."

But the young man did not return. It has now been six years and Romero gazes upon the book, The Shadow of the Wind, still being held with a tag bearing the name of Dan Semper. Maybe True Grit was the only book for this young man, or maybe he's gone digital? Romero didn't know. He put the book back down. He would wait a little longer.

The first cold night of the season arrived later than usual in Colorado, but when it came everything froze solid. The train was late and people huddled. The bookshop was warm compared to the cold outside and Romero had a steady stream of readers. He sold a few *Gone Girls,* a Harry Potter, and a Stephen King. This was nice. This was good business.

After the Stephen King customer made his purchase and left the store, Romero glanced above the cash register. He couldn't believe his eyes. It was him, the young man, coming into the bookshop! Well, he wasn't so young anymore, but still so much the same. This man, this Dan Semper, sighted Romero but didn't seem to recognize him. Romero was unfazed. "Hey, kid, you've come back! It's been a long time but you've come back, just like I knew you would."

"Come back?" said Semper. "Come back from what? I don't think I've ever been here before."

"But of course you have," said Romero. "Look, I've got your book."

"My book? What book?"

"I was holding it for you. You remember, The Shadow of the Wind? You were going to return and pick it up."

"I don't know about that."

"You are Semper, correct?"

"I am Semper."

"You are Dan Semper, correct?"

"I am Dan Semper."

"Then I have your book. Would you like me to ring it up now, or would you prefer to do more shopping?"

"Wait," said Semper. "I'm feeling funny. *If* this happened, it happened a long time ago. You've been holding it for me all these years?"

"Yes. I want you to read the book and then I want you to go to Barcelona."

"But I've already been to Barcelona."

"Without reading the book? Dan!"

"I forgot about the book."

"What about the paella?" asked Romero. "Did you eat the paella? What did you think of the paella?"

"It was okay."

"Okay? Dan, you ate the beach paella, didn't you?"

"Well, we were already at the beach. And it looked really good in the photo they had."

"Tourist paella. Poor Dan. You'll just have to go back and do it again."

"Listen, this is all very strange, but I'll go ahead and buy the book. I don't really remember the book, but I'll buy the book. It was so kind of you to save it for me."

"If you don't want it," said Romero, "at least pass it on to Julian. I think he's almost ready for a book such as this."

"Julian? What about Julian? That's my son. How do you know of my son?"

"It's all in the book, Daniel, *The Shadow of the Wind*. You really should get around to reading it some day."

Dan Semper left the store with book in hand. He was a hard sell, Romero thought, a hard sell indeed. But no man lives by True Grit alone, at least not in his bookshop.

The Picnic: A Story of Celery

**The story you are about to read is partially true. Though the names have been changed, the vegetable remains pristine.

The *D league* women's volleyball season ended with a picnic. It was a losing season, yes, but the picnic went a long way to sooth any hurts. Two of the five member team brought significant others. There was plenty of beer, cider, fruit, cheese, and chips to go around. After all, who doesn't love a picnic?

But all good things come to an end, and when dusk approached one of the couples called it quits. Marion and Boris gathered their things and said their good-byes. Betty, the team's captain, called to them. "Hey, why don't you take home some of this beer?"

Boris politely declined Betty's offer, but held up a plastic baggie filled with fresh celery sticks. "Do you mind if I take home some of this celery instead? I really love celery. In fact, they call me the celery man."

"Take all you want, celery man," said Betty. "I bought tons at Costco."

"Maybe I should go home with you then?" Boris replied.

"Hey, watch it, buster!" laughed Marion.

The remaining players watched Boris and Marion walk away, but the two made it only as far as the parking lot. From seemingly out of nowhere, a man leaped out between the parked cars and confronted them with a gun. "Look, take what you want," said a panicked Boris. "We don't want any trouble."

"I don't want any trouble either," said the gunman, calmly. "I just want the celery. Just hand over the celery and nobody gets hurt. Got it?"

Boris reluctantly parted with the baggie and the gunman took off like a rocket. Marion, with Boris in tow, scurried back to the safety of the picnic. The other players rose nervously as they saw looks of exasperation in the faces of their friends.

"What's happened?" asked Betty.

"We were robbed!" replied Marion.

"That's awful," said Betty. "I mean, right here in the park."

"But we were lucky," said Boris. "All he wanted was the celery. Imagine that, robbing a guy of his celery?"

"I think I've heard of that guy," said Forrest, Betty's husband. "They call him *'The Celery Kid.'* You really have to watch yourself at picnics."

"Well, I hate to ask this," said Boris to Betty, "but have you any more of the celery? That evil doer really cleaned me out."

Betty turned over all the remaining celery to Boris while Forrest reported to the police. Once Boris and Marion exited a second time, Betty remarked that years ago someone would have gladly taken home all the beer and not cared a wit about a bag of celery. "What's next?" asked Betty to the gathered team, "A thief of kale, *'The Kale Rider?'*"

Santa Fe highway was crowded in early evening, and the police were soon closing in on The Celery Kid and his bright green getaway car. And though it went against his every instinct, the Kid tossed the celery out his window. Now he had nothing left to lose and could afford to be reckless. And he did elude the police. He rode on to rob and pillage again.

Responding police officers did find the baggie along a ditch near Mineral Avenue. Officer Pete raised his hand in caution. "Wait, don't touch anything. It's evidence."

"Jeez, Pete," said officer Joe. "It's just a bag of celery. Don't make a federal case of it."

"Well, in that case," said officer Pete, "I'd like to take it home with me. I sure do enjoy a good stalk of celery from time to time."

"I say we split it even," said officer Joe. "I know my celery and this is good stuff. Look at that color. Look at those lines."

Officer Pete and officer Joe divided the celery and took it home. Forrest took home the beer while Betty and the others gathered the rest. Volleyball season was indeed over, but not without a story to tell.

The Crisis

Kendall thought she recognized the man who came into the bar, but that was happening a lot lately now that the crisis was over and people were returning to the city. She made a beeline for the man before he could even belly up to the bar. "Where do I know you from?" Kendall asked him. "I think I've seen you somewhere."

"I have no idea," the man replied, startled, "but you look familiar to me as well."

"I used to dance on stage," said Kendall. "Maybe that's where you've seen me? Often times people have seen me dance on stage. It's what I used to do. I danced."

"Yes, of course, you were with the Poo-poo-pee-doo Review!"

"Oh, no," she said. "That's not it at all. Those girls were our rivals. My name is Kendall Oliver. I was with the Dancing Donnas. Do you remember the Dancing Donnas? We were the ones. We stood out."

"No, I'm sorry," he said. "I don't remember the Dancing Donnas. It was my mistake."

"What about you?" Kendall asked. "What did you do before…"

"I was a writer," he said, proudly. "Maybe you…"

"Yes, for the Tribune! They had your picture…"

"No," he corrected her, "not the Tribune. I was with the Times. Did you ever read the Times?"

"No, I didn't read that one," Kendall admitted. "I was a Trib girl through and through. Gosh, are we not a pair of scatterbrains?"

He laughed at her remark and then offered to buy her a drink, which Kendall readily accepted. They each grabbed a stool and hoisted themselves up against the bar. He told her his name was Jack, and that he was with the second wave that returned to the city. Kendall searched her memory for anyone named Jack who used to be a writer but kept coming up empty. Still, she thought him awfully handsome and he seemed kind enough. She told him she was drinking vodka; he was a gin man. The bartender caught his eye and came over. Jack placed their order.

The bartender appeared to be in her late twenties, tall and thin with jet-black hair. Jack noticed her sleeves rolled all the way down to her hands and her shirt buttoned up as high as it could go. He thought she might be covering up scars or burn marks or perhaps a mixture of the two; they all seemed to be covering up something these days.

"Do you like her?" Kendall asked him.

"What?"

"I mean, do you think she's pretty, the bartender?"

"Why yes," Jack replied, "she's very pretty, though I didn't mean to take notice. I was rude to you."

"No, it's okay, really," Kendall assured him. "Listen, I may be presumptuous here, but if we party later, away from here, I might be able to get her to come along. I hear she's great fun. She might be up for it, for whatever."

"Whew, that's a fine thought," said Jack, a nervous laugh escaping his lips. "But, you see, I haven't been out for quite some time. I really think I ought to take it slow."

"Yes, take it slow," Kendall replied, "but not too slow. Life is short you know."

The hot bartender returned with their drink order. She and Kendall made small talk while Jack nursed his gin. He was happy now, this moment, and it had been so long since he 'd felt anything close to that particular emotion. He could feel himself smiling and it felt so strange. It was as if the muscles in his face had nearly lost the ability to do that anymore and now this — a smile, albeit a sad kind of smile as if he were a clown. Maybe he was a clown, he thought, as he twirled his gin around, sitting there like a fool with these younger women at a bar. But aside from the girls, the possibilities, it was something else. He felt good being out in public again, relaxing while savoring a drink, listening to the music. Music again, sweet music. It was good enough for him. It was so damn good, really.

Kendall then asked Jack if he was married. "Sort of," he said, sheepishly.

"Uh-oh, I know what that means."

"No, it's not like that," Jack said to her. "Terry never came back to the city with me, with the second wave. She joined up with the missionaries instead. She said she just couldn't come back and start all over."

"The missionaries," said Kendall, aghast. "That can be dangerous work."

"I know. I haven't heard from her in quite some time, and I can't even get a message through. I don't know where she is. I don't know anything. I was just tired of sitting at home night after night staring at the walls."

"You have kids?" she asked.

"We did."

"Oh, I'm so sorry," said Kendall.

"It's okay. There are so many of us in the same situation, some way worse."

"But it doesn't make it hurt any less," she offered. "I'm glad you're out tonight. It's too painful to hide yourself away, to stare at the walls as you've said."

Jack took a big swallow of gin. "What about you, Kendall? Are you married as well?"

"You can put me down as *sort of married* as well," she said with a laugh. "Hank and I have an understanding."

"And just what is that understanding?" he asked her.

"That I go out from time to time when I need to."

"What about Hank?" Jack inquired. "What does he do?"

"Hank doesn't go out."

"Is he okay?"

"No, he's not" Kendall admitted. "But it's not so much a physical thing for him, it's mental. Hank can't go out. He does other things."

Kendall and Jack stopped speaking but smiled at each other, sadly, before returning to their drinks. This happened a lot. One person's pain smashes into the pain of another and they both come crashing down. This is the kind of thing they were trying to avoid. "Another drink, Jack?" asked Kendall, breaking the silence. "Fuck it, I'm buying."

They drank enough to get tipsy, lost the bartender to the throngs, and then retreated to Jack's place. It was no great shakes, his apartment, but it was ten stories high so you could really see the city. He let Kendall take in the view of the night. "Wow, look at all those lights, Jack! People are really coming back to the city. They're really coming back."

Jack agreed. "It seems there are more and more lights every night. Soon it will be normal again, or whatever counts as normal these days." He took Kendall by the hand and led her to his bedroom. She went right to the window and peered out at the lights again, her eyes ablaze, as if seeing stars for the first time. Jack sat on the bed still holding her hand, afraid to let go, afraid she might leave him to another night alone. "I want you, Kendall," he whispered to her. "I'm so glad you're here with me."

"You sure the wife won't be back?"

"I don't even think she knows where I live."

"There's another thing, Jack. You have to know that I'm damaged goods."

"What? You're so beautiful."

Kendall's eyes went dull. She lost her smile. "Do you know that I was bought and sold two times over? I was another's legal possession as an adult. Can you even believe that?"

"I believe it because I know those stories are true. I just can't fathom it because it didn't happen to me."

"There's a chip implanted in my brain to this day. I asked the doctor to take it out, but he says he can't because it might kill me to do so. I told him to go ahead with that but he didn't think that was so funny. So I have this chip inside my head. Who knows what it'll do to me? Who knows what it's already done?"

"We don't have to do this, Kendall, if it's too painful, if you're not ready."

"Yes, we do. We have to do this. I *need* to do this. Please, Jack. I have to feel something besides pain. Hell, I'll even take the pain. I have to feel something. I just have to. Please, anything. Please."

He kissed her hand. "It's okay."

Kendall began unbuttoning her blouse. "Could you dim the lights, Jack?"

"I'll turn them off."

"I used to love undressing for Hank. He loved it too. That much I could tell. Now it's different because I have scars and cuts and other things. I'm a little disfigured you could say. Well, maybe a lot disfigured."

"It's all right, Kendall. It's fine with me. I haven't seen a woman in quite some time."

"In the dark it's all right, Jack. In the light I'm Frankenstein. That's the way it is now. That's the way it will always be." Her blouse and bra were now discarded, and then her pants and underwear came off as well. "There," she said, covering herself as best she could. "I hope you're okay with me."

"Come here."

"This would be way easier if I didn't like you, Jack."

"It won't be easy for either of us, Kendall. I don't think it ever will be again. But why don't we just kiss and this will be where we'll start. We'll start over again right now."

Kendall leaned over and kissed him, deeply, hungrily. Jack returned her kiss in kind, and as he touched her, he could feel scar tissue along her flank. He couldn't help feeling her scars; they were everywhere. What he could see in the dim light startled him. On her buttocks was some sort of numerical branding along with stark redness and what looked like serrated whip marks. One of her breasts was seemingly deflated and the nipple was missing as well. The other was stretched and discolored. Her back and legs had similar wounds. Damaged goods? Frankenstein? He was shocked that she was alive at all.

Jack pulled Kendall down onto the bed and then stood up to undress as well. After he finished she looked up at him, astonished not by what she saw but what she didn't see. "Turn around please," she said.

"What?"

"My God, there's not a scratch on you. How'd you manage that? It's like you're… pristine."

"Oh, you noticed," said Jack. "The thing is, when all this was happening we had to race to make it to the underground. It was horrible. I mean, when the bombs began exploding and we couldn't find the kids. But it's true I didn't get a scratch on me. So many times I considered shooting myself in the foot, the leg, anywhere. But I hear if you get caught as a fake it could really go bad for you. So I'm stuck. All of you are Frankensteins and yet I'm the freak."

"Don't complain and count your blessings," said Kendall.

"I know. I'm sorry."

"We tried to make it to the underground, Hank and I, but we just came up short, ran out of time. And then, well, it was all over. Eventually Hank couldn't stand the pain of it all, the ugliness, and retreated into his head. I envied him for this. I wanted to retreat myself but couldn't do it. So I listened to the screams, watched with disgust, felt the pain, the unbearable pain. Why couldn't I detach? I wanted to so badly."

"I think it's because you're strong, Kendall. You must be so strong-willed."

"No, I don't consider it strength at all. I commanded my body to die when all this happened but it wouldn't. It's cowardly. I was afraid to die, completely afraid."

"There's no cowardice in wanting to live, Kendall. You love life, that's all. You have so much more to give. That's what I believe."

"Okay, stop making me feel better. It's dark, I'm horny. Can we get this thing going here? I've still got some parts in fine working order."

Jack began touching her, and what was initially awkward soon became something akin to natural. He found a rhythm with her movement and it felt so good to him. This perfect night with this damaged person. He momentarily forgot about his own damage, his inner damage, his great losses. Oh God, his wife was somewhere out there and his children were never coming back. They're dead, just dead. All he had now was Kendall, this girl he'd just met, this girl he was now having sex with. Sex, my gosh, was it really happening? He couldn't hold on any longer. Soon after finishing his mood went dark. He said to her, "What about your children, Kendall? Did you have any children? Do you miss them?"

"No, no children," replied Kendall, rolling away from him. "It was the one thing they couldn't take away from us. I'm so sorry, Jack. I can see that you're really hurting."

"I'm just so damn sad, and happy too at the same time. I think the happy part is because you're here with me, Kendall. I'm really thankful for you."

"I want you to talk to Hank. You'll come over to our place and talk to Hank. He's worse off than I am but he's good to talk to, Jack, and that's what you need. You'll like Hank. He's a good man. You'll be fast friends and we'll build something. Who knows what, but we'll build something and become regular people again. I know it. Look at all the lights out there and tell me I'm wrong. So many lights, so many people coming home."

"Gosh," said Jack, "I guess we never did figure out if we knew each other before this thing happened, the crisis."

"No," she replied. "What we are is a new beginning…and I like that."

The Barney 5

It played like a mantra running through his brain. *Sell the decision makers…Sell the decision makers…* And this is just what Tobey Sutton intended to do as he bounded up the corporate steps of MAS Industries with a briefcase chock full of samples. He was a salesman after all, though a bit down on his luck. Today would be different, he thought. Today is a great day to die, and it's also a great day to live. He was happy. He was confident.

Once inside the nearly empty glass building, Tobey approached the first person he could find. It was a man filling up his coffee mug in what looked to be a break station. "Are you the decision maker for MAS Industries?" he asked the man whose glasses nearly fell from his face.

"Are you kidding me?" he replied. "I can't even decide what I want for lunch. Do I want tacos? Do I want pizza? I don't know. You should ask Kara. She makes some decisions."

"That's wonderful," said Tobey. "Where is this Kara?"

The man pointed down the hall and off went Tobey. He found a woman busy with filing or some other such task. "Are you Kara?" he asked her.

"Who wants to know?"

"Tobey Sutton wants to know and that's me. I hear you make the decisions around here."

"I do make decisions," said Kara, "but only with regards to lunch. Nobody can decide on what they're having, so I make those decisions for them. Now what can I help you with Mr. Sutton?"

"I was really hoping to find the decision maker, because I've got some really great products to show. You won't believe…"

"Stop right there, Sutton. Unless you've got some lunch ideas I can't help you. You'll have to see Barney."

"Barney? Who is Barney?"

"Barney is who you go through for just about everything in this place," said Kara. "If you can get something past Barney, well, good luck to you."

"What's his last name?" asked Tobey. "I'd be happy to meet him."

"He ain't got one. He's just Barney. That's all you need to know, Mr. Sutton."

"Where can I find this Barney?"

Kara pointed even farther down the hall, to the very end in fact. Tobey squared his shoulders and charged down the corridor. He didn't want to lose any of his confidence. I'll show this Barney what I've got, he thought. I'll show him.

At the end of the hall was a door without a name, room number, or any indication that it was somebody's office. It may have been a custodial closet for all Tobey knew. Warily, he knocked upon the door. There was no answer so he tried it again at greater volume. This time he distinctly heard the word 'enter.' Tobey slowly pushed the door open and glanced inside. There was a man seated behind a desk, an ordinary man about his age, but no other furniture except for a plain folding chair in front of the desk. There were no wall decorations, pictures, paintings, or anything on the desk itself but a computer. It was easily the most boring office Tobey had ever seen and he'd seen a lot of them. There wasn't even a window. "Are you Barney?" said Tobey.

"Yes, I am."

"I hate to be so informal at a business meeting," said Tobey. "May I have your last name?"

"My last name is 5."

"Five," repeated Tobey. "Spelled like the number five?"

"Sort of," said Barney. "But it's actually 5, the numerical 5. I'm the fifth edition of the Barney series. I'm a robot. Barney number 5. Now what can I help you with?"

"Wow, you look so real. I would never have guessed."

"We Barneys do fool a lot of people."

"Are you the decision maker?" asked Tobey.

"Yes, as a matter of fact I am. I make all the decisions for MAS Industries."

"Except for lunch."

Barney 5 laughed, or whatever passed for laughter among robots. "Yes, except for lunch. Those chumps can eat dog food for all I care."

"Okay," said Tobey, "I don't care what they're having for lunch either. What I wanted to do was introduce myself. I'm Tobey Sutton, and I want to sell to MAS Industries some wonderful products I've brought along with me today."

"No," said Barney.

"No? But you haven't even seen them."

"I'm sorry, Tobey Sutton, but your products are neither needed nor wanted. I'm a robot. I've seen them all. It's been a pleasure to meet you."

"But they slice," said Tobey.

"No."

"And they dice."

"No."

"They're self-cleaning," pleaded Tobey.

"I don't care."

"They're self-starting."

"Big whoop."

"They're energy efficient."

"Who cares…"

"Please," said Tobey. "What can I do to convince you how great these products are? Is it me? Do you not like me?"

"No," said Barney, "I like you just fine."

"Listen," said Tobey, "I'll do anything. I'm really down on my luck here. You name it. I'll do anything."

"No you won't."

"I will," said Tobey. "You try me. I will."

"All right, Tobey Sutton," said Barney, "I'll try you. At this moment I am prepared to buy 100,000 units of your product."

"Right now?" questioned Tobey. "But I haven't even taken them out of my briefcase."

"Oh, I'm sure they're fine."

"100,000 units? Have you any idea how large a commission I'd get for 100,000 units?"

"Yes Tobey, I know exactly how much of a commission you'd get."

"I'd be a legend back at the office."

"Yes, you would," said Barney.

"I'd be practically set for life."

"Indeed, you would."

"But what's the catch?" inquired Tobey. "There's got to be catch here."

"I do have one simple request," replied Barney. "In return for MAS Industries buying 100,000 units, I want you to do one simple thing: I want you to kill me."

"*Kill you*!" exclaimed Tobey. "But you said you were a robot. You're not even alive. How can I kill you?"

"Well, not exactly kill me per say, but I'll give you a special code and you'll turn me off — for good. I'm not programmed to do this myself."

"But I'll be caught…and punished."

"Not a chance," said Barney. "I'll set the timer so this happens one or two weeks from now. I'll erase everything pertinent. They'll never trace it back to you. It'd be impossible."

"Listen, Barney, I'm just a salesman, and not even a very good one. I don't know if I want to get caught up in any of this."

"Tobey, I wouldn't even ask you except that you're my best friend."

"*Best friend*? We just met, Barney."

"Yes, but I told you that I liked you, and I don't like anybody else. So you must be my best friend."

"Barney, this is asking a lot."

"Tobey, do you have a girlfriend or a wife?"

"I do have a girl, Shirley as a matter of fact."

"Well, I don't have a girlfriend, a wife, and aside from you not a single friend. Now what about the weekend? You and Shirley have plans?"

"Maybe we do, though certainly nothing extravagant."

"Well, I don't" said Barney, "extravagant or otherwise. I sit here in the dark. In fact, that's what happens when everybody else goes home for the day. I sit here in the dark. I don't have anything or anybody. I'm nothing, Tobey. And do you think any of those flubs out there in the office care about me? They don't. Do you know they used to throw things at me until I started docking their pay. One of them plays computer games at his desk all day. Another hides alcohol in the men's room. And that girl out there's a floozy. I caught her on an on-line dating service and she's married. She tried to re-boot me, and I almost gave her the physical boot except that I'm not programmed for violence. You see, they hate me because I'm the decision maker. But it's guys like us, Tobey, you and me, who hold things together. We're the ones who move things along. Not those dullards."

"You're really in a bad way, too," said Tobey. "Is it possible I could just kidnap you or something?"

"No, I way a ton. Literally, I weigh a ton. I'm not going anywhere. But I tell you what, they will get me out of here as soon as the Barney 6 is introduced. I don't know when that's coming but coming it is. I'd much rather go out on my own terms. Just let me stick it to them one time. Let me make the one decision that really counts, the one I can't do on my own."

"I just can't help you," said Tobey. "I'm sorry."

"Listen, I'll write a program that'll be indispensable to the Barney 6. That way some little piece of the Barney 5 will be within the Barney 6. I'll recognize you. And after buying 100,000 units I think the two of us are going to do a lot of business together. What do you say, buddy? You're my friend. I wouldn't ask this of anyone else. What do you say?"

"Oh golly," said Tobey. "Oh gosh darn. Are you sure we'll see each other again? I could sure use a friend sometimes."

"Absolutely. Hey, we're not only friends, we're best buds. We'll have a lot of catching up to do. I want to hear all about Shirley. And you did say you'd do anything…"

"Gee whiz, the things I do for my friends…"

Barney opened his shirt for Tobey, revealing a box within his chest that had a key pad. "Just punch in the number 19650314. And hey, guess what? Your sale just went through. You're a rich man, Tobey Sutton. I'll be seeing you on the flip side."

Tobey punched in the numbers as directed. "Good-bye, my friend. Good-bye, Barney number 5."

So Now What?

Stan nudged his truck into a parking spot at Jesse Turner's. He liked coming to this sports bar for the most part, dropping by whenever he had some time to kill and some beers to drink. Once inside, he settled onto a barstool and ordered a beer. On the television screen above was a west coast college football game. Stan didn't follow either team but watched the play regardless. He wasn't really thinking though, not thinking about anything. Someone else had sidled up on the next barstool over. Stan hadn't noticed until he was spoken to. "You drink with your pinky finger extended," Stan heard a voice say to him.

"What?"

"It's a feminine affectation you understand."

"What is?" said Stan.

"Drinking with your pinky extended," said the man.

Stan didn't know what to make of the man's comment but tucked back his pinky just the same. It was now glued to his glass.

"I didn't mean to insult you," the man said to Stan.

"I wasn't insulted."

"I mean, you can drink your beer however you'd like. Don't take my comment as anything."

Stan turned and regarded his neighbor. The man wasn't tall, he wasn't wide. He really wasn't anything worthy of intimidation at all. Stan could certainly take him — if he had to, if he wanted to. "Look, man," said Stan, "I just came in here for a beer, okay? I don't know why you're looking at my hands anyway."

"I wasn't looking at you hands, I was looking at your finger."

"What about my finger?" asked Stan.

"I already told you."

Stan leaned closer to the man so he could speak and be heard in a softer voice. "Buddy, I hope you know this is a sports bar and not a gay bar. I hope you're not trying to pick me up or anything."

"I know it's not a gay bar," said the man. "I'm not gay."

"Let's just drink our beer," Stan muttered.

"You should drink lots, it's free for you."

"Why's that?" asked Stan.

"It's ladies' night."

Stan spun around and grabbed the man by his shirt collar. They were both off their bar stools at this point with Stan hovering over the fallen man and staring menacingly into his eyes. "What'd you say to me?" growled Stan.

"Let me go. I didn't mean anything."

The bartender rushed over and separated the two men. They adjusted themselves and returned to their stools. "He's trying to get a rise out of me and I don't know why," said Stan to the bartender.

"Next time take it outside," the bartender replied. "Now you two kiss and make up."

The two men reluctantly shook hands. The other man then introduced himself as Barry and offered to buy Stan a drink. They drank in mostly silence, any small talk stayed on safe topics. When Stan rose from his stool to leave the bar, Barry once again extended his hand. "No hard feelings, okay?"

"No hard feelings," Stan agreed.

The next day Stan called Ronnie, his best friend since grade school. He told Ronnie about the past evening and his near fight with Barry. Ronnie laughed at the absurdity of it all, noting that not all women drink with their pinky fingers extended anyway. "You know what, you should have just whipped out your dick right then and there. That would have shut him up."

"I don't need to do that," Stan replied. "I know who I am."

"Well, if you know who you are then it shouldn't have upset you. I would have told him to just fuck off and die."

"You have more of a way with words than I do," said Stan.

Later that day Stan went over to visit his parents. He sat with his mother at the kitchen table. "The guy thought I was a woman. Do you believe that, mom? We almost got into a fight."

"A fight? Oh, heavens. He doesn't know how special you are."

"What's that supposed to mean, mom?"

"Nothing. You've just always been my special little guy is all. Different from all the others."

"Mom?"

Stan found his father puttering around in the garage. "Dad, you have three sons, right? Me and my two brothers, right?"

"That's what I tell anyone who asks."

"What do you mean, dad?"

"I do have three sons. That's my story and I'll take it with me to the grave."

"Dad?"

That night Stan took a good look at himself in the mirror. He wondered what Barry had seen in him. Sure, he was good looking, but a woman? Stan slowly undressed and then took at look at the mirror once again. This time he saw something else. This time he saw the truth.

Stan put his clothes back on. He had a few drinks and then called Ronnie again. He asked Ronnie if there was anything he could do that might jeopardize their friendship. Ronnie assured Stan that as long as he didn't abuse women, kids, or animals, there was nothing that could upset their friendship. That's when Stan admitted to Ronnie that he was indeed a woman.

"Well, you're going to have to change your first name I would think."

"Ronnie, I'm not kidding. I really am a woman."

"Because a guy in a bar told you that? I sure hope he doesn't tell you to jump off a cliff."

Stan reminded Ronnie that his sage advice was to whip out his dick. Stan told Ronnie that there was no dick to whip out. "There's nothing there, Ronnie. Nothing."

"Well, there's got to be something down there."

"I can assure you it's not a dick."

"You'll talk to my wife, Stan. I mean, she's had a vagina…like her whole life. You talk to her and then you'll transition, or not transition, or whatever you want to do. It's a process, right? And we'll be with you every step of the way. You're not getting rid of old Ronnie that easily. We'll still be pals, okay? Nothing changes."

Stan returned to the sports bar every night until he ran into Barry. He said to him, "About that crack about ladies' night…"

"I really am sorry, Stan. I was way out of line. It won't happen again."

"No, Barry, don't be. Don't be sorry because, well, it happens to be the truth."

"You really are a lady?"

"I really am," said Stan. "So now what?"

It's Alright, Ma (I'm Only Levitating)

Greg returned home after a long day at work to his wife, Alma, and their newborn daughter, Gina. Only Gina was nowhere to be found. A panicked Greg said to Alma, "Honey, where's the baby?" Alma said nothing, but pointed up at the ceiling.

"What the?" said an aghast Greg as he gazed up at his diapered baby hovering gently near the ceiling.

"She's been up there nearly an hour," said Alva. "I can't get her to come down. I think she's actually sleeping."

"Well," said Greg, scratching his head, "sleeping or no sleeping, the ceiling is no place for a baby."

"Hey," said Alma, "I'll feed the baby and I'll change the baby, but I won't be peeling her off the ceiling for you. That'll be your job, buddy."

"Fair enough," replied Greg. "Fair enough. I'll go fetch the ladder. You call Dr. Hobbs. This is all highly irregular."

Greg carefully retrieved Gina from the ceiling, then all three raced to Dr. Hobbs' office. Once inside, the doctor asked Greg and Alma why they'd brought little Gina in. Greg said nothing while Alma released the baby from her grasp. Rather than falling to the floor, Gina simply levitated at about eye level to the adults in the room.

"By golly you've got a floater!" said old Doc Hobbs. "Why I haven't seen one of these in years," he said while casually waving his hand beneath the levitating baby. "I'll be darned…"

"But what do we do?" asked Greg.

"What do you do?" laughed the doctor. "What do you do? You don't do anything is what you do. Enjoy the spectacle I guess."

Dr. Hobbs inquired as to whether Greg and Alma were first time parents. They were. He them counseled them not to panic, that although floaters were a rarity for sure, they were not entirely unheard of. He informed the frightened parents that Gina was small and light even for a baby, and that gases had simply built up inside her and caused her to levitate. She would eventually burp and fart and return on her own to the safety of their arms. Dr. Hobbs relayed that he had seen some floaters in the past climb down the curtains themselves when they were hungry enough. "They always return to the boob, right Greg?" said the doctor with a wink in his eye. "Am I right?"

"What are you asking me for?" replied Greg. "I've never heard of such a thing."

"Seriously," said the doctor, "it's nothing to worry about. Just make sure to keep her tethered if you take her outside, and keep watch for birds of prey. Otherwise, she'll be fine. Fine I say. Why I once had a floater that made it clear over to Omaha before we got him back down to solid earth. Now that boy was some kind of floater, some kind of floater indeed. They don't make them like that anymore."

"Hey, I bet my Gina could make it past Omaha," said Greg, proudly.

"Now you're talking!" Doc Hobbs replied. "That's the spirit I like to hear."

In the end, Gina floated for two more seasons until she put some weight on her and never took that kind of flight again. But every now and then her parents keep one eye on the sky, and bid a sigh of relief every time a belch escapes from Gina's tiny body.

Cupid

They lowered him into the ground, someone said a few words, and that was that. But I couldn't concentrate on any of the proceedings as my mind wandered back to a story about this man, this man when he was alive. Oh, he was a live one all right.

Jobs back then didn't have fancy titles such as Special Assistant Programmer II or Graphic Design Launch Profiler. I was hired by Mr. Ketchavarian to simply 'help him with the things he needed help with.' So I answered his phone, filed some papers, spiffed up the office, anything really, anything that helped. Mr. Ketchavarian was from a country I hadn't heard of as I had then little interest in geography or culture. He didn't care to talk about it either. If anyone pressed him about the old country, he would just tell them "What does it matter about any of that? I'm in this country now. Now is what matters."

One of the ways I could assist him was with his English lessons. He went to night school once a week and made steady progress. His accent was thick though, and he had a difficult time picking up slang and some other words and expressions most of us took for granted. He'd practice with me either before class or the day after. Practice, was, well, interesting. As I'm able to recall, our conversation went something like this. "You are a man liker," he bluntly told me. "You like many men."

"I'm a Humanist," I corrected him. "We like everybody."

"But why do you like all these men?" he asked.

"Men and women. Humans. We believe in human potential. We believe we can live in a world without religion, live in a world with mutual respect for all."

"That's just stupid," he spat. "Let me tell you, you don't know your ass from your face.

You have an ass, you have a face, but you know they have switched positions. That is what I believe. Yes, I do."

"Mr. Ketchavarian, with all due respect, your only position is to insult mine. Now please, let's get back to our lessons."

"Yes, Frank, let us get back to our lessons. There is a word I would like you to define for me. Here, you can see I've written it down for you."

"Oh, no. Sorry. I'm not reading that," I told him.

"Oh yes you are, Frank. You will read this word to me and then you will define it. Otherwise, they will kick me out of this country."

"I can assure you, Mr. Ketchavarian, you will not be kicked out of the country because of this word."

"It's true, they will kick me out. They are very strict these people. In that case, I won't have a country and you won't have a job. Now come now, Frank. Read this word to me. I depend on you."

I couldn't tell whether he was messing with me or not. He probably was, but what could I do? I needed the job and the job was, quite frankly, easy money. "Okay, Mr. Ketchavarian, I will read you this word. The word is: Dildo."

"Dildo? Is that how you say it? That's a funny thing to say, is it not?"

"Yes, it's hilarious. Dildo."

"You must tell me, Frank, what is this dildo?"

"Mr. Ketchavarian, we did this with the word *shit* last week."

"Yes, I remember this shit you say. That's so funny to me when you say it."

"You're doing this at my expense, to laugh at me, to make fun. I don't think you're interested in these lessons at all."

"Frank, please. I must have a passing grade. You must tell me the definition of this word. It's very important. Please."

"A dildo is a substitute for a penis, Mr. Ketchavarian. I'm sure your teacher will be very impressed that you know this."

"But why would you need a substitute. Why would you not use the real thing?"

"I don't know. I suppose if the real thing isn't working then you might need a substitute."

"Tell me, Frank. Where is yours? Where is this dildo that you are keeping?"

"I'm afraid I don't have one."

"Are you telling me, Frank, that you left your dildo at home?"

"I'm telling you, Mr. Ketchavarian, that I don't have one. Period."

"If it's in your car you can go get it. I very much wish to see this dildo that you are keeping."

"Well, you can't see it because it doesn't exist. And I think you understand exactly what I'm saying to you."

So we practiced saying dildo a few more times and then inserted the word into proper sentences. Our lesson devolved soon after and then appeared to be over. Mr. Ketchavarian snapped his notebook shut and looked me straight in the eye. "Tell me, Frank, your home is for you alone. Is that right to say? You go home and then you are alone, correct?"

"I do live alone. I am single if that's what you mean."

"This is sad to me, Frank. It's sad to me that you have nobody."

"It's not a sad situation, Mr. Ketchavarian. I do have friends. I do go on dates sometimes. Not many."

"Are you talking about these Humanist men you cavort with?"

"I do not cavort with Humanist men."

He studied my face longer than I was comfortable with. I would have loved to get back to the English lessons, but could tell he wasn't done with his probing yet. "Frank, I must ask you something that is very important."

"Please don't."

"Frank, this is important. You must listen."

"Okay, I'm listening."

"Have you now, Frank, or have you ever, been a fan of this disco music?"

"Disco music? Are you kidding me? That's important for you to know?"

"It's very important, Frank. I must know this about you."

"No, Mr. Ketchavarian, I do not like disco music."

"But you did before, right? You were a disco king?"

"I was not a disco king! What the hell? I rocked hard. Ask anybody from my high school."

"Well, you know, we all tell ourselves lies."

"I'm not lying, Mr. Ketchavarian. I do not like disco. I never have."

"Frank, please. It would help me…for my lessons…if you would please read out loud a sentence that I have written especially for you. I will get my tape machine."

I silently read his sentence while he prepared his *tape machine*. "You've got to be kidding me," I said to him. "You're demented."

"Frank, you must read this out loud so I can practice later with the tape machine. You must, please."

So here's what I read aloud to him. *"I love disco music. I love to shake my booty. I am, Frank, the disco king of all!* And what about dildo? Don't you want to hear that, too? *Dildo! Dildo! Dildo!"*

"No, I just wanted to hear the disco part."

The office door opened just as Mr. Ketchavarian turned off his tape machine. Are you ever prepared when the most beautiful girl you've ever seen enters a room and stands just five feet in front of your face? This after proclaiming myself disco king of all. No, I couldn't move, couldn't speak. I heard Mr. Ketchavarian greeting his niece, Ekaterina, and then in a fog speaking to me. "You know Ekaterina loves this disco music. It is disco, disco, disco, all night long. And what's funny is that Frank here was just telling me how much love he has for this disco. Isn't that right, Frank?"

Ekaterina's eyes lit up like fireworks. And now I believe in love at first sight. I truly believe it. I believe! I believe!

"Yes," I said, my eyes locked on Ekaterina. "I do love disco…with all my heart. In fact, we even have it on tape. Don't we, Mr. Ketchavarian?"

"That is correct, Frank. The tape does not tell a lie. And now it seems to me two disco lovers should not be in a stuffy office. You should be taking over the disco floor, Frank!"

With that he took out a Red Lobster gift certificate and placed it on my palm. I took Ekaterina out then, and it's many years later and she's still with me now. In fact, she's holding my hand as we walk across the damp cemetery grass. That's just one story I've told you about our uncle, Mikhal Ketchavarian, our Cupid and my friend. He will be missed.

Tuborg, The Runt of the Litter

The big day had finally come. It was adoption day for Miss Applebutter's seven little puppies. They were all brothers and sisters and eager for their forever homes. From biggest to smallest they were as follows: Jocko, Hildy, Leslie, Pablo, Reese, Cookie, Wayne, and — really a half-puppy because he was so small — Tuborg, the runt of the litter.

"You may have to stay here with Miss Applebutter," said Leslie to Tuborg. "Who would want to adopt such a scrawny, little puppy?"

"Miss Applebutter says it's what's on the inside that counts," replied Tuborg. "And I've got a lot going on inside me."

"Well, I hope so," said Jocko, "because there ain't much on the outside that I can see."

"I'll show you," said Tuborg. "I'll get adopted. Just you wait."

And wait he did. For once the adoption began, all six of Tuborg's siblings found their forever homes. It was getting late in the evening and Tuborg found himself all alone at the feet of Miss Applebutter. "Don't you worry, Tuborg," she said to him. "You'll always have a home here if nobody else comes round."

"I know," said Tuborg. "I was just hoping so much to be adopted."

The sun was just about to set for the night and poor Tuborg still waited by the door. Just then, a thundering knock startled the whole house. "Who could that be?" asked Miss Applebutter. "I thought the adoption was over for the day."

She opened the door to a big, burly older man with an unlit cigar clenched between his teeth. The coat he wore was thick and long like that of a wooly mammoth. He towered above Miss Applebutter and little Tuborg rose just above his ankles. "I hear you got some puppies up for adoption," said the giant man.

"Well, we did earlier," admitted Miss Applebutter. "But I'm afraid they've all been adopted — except for little Tuborg here."

"Tuborg you say," said the large man. "And you're telling me that's a dog?"

"Of course I'm a dog!" protested Tuborg.

"Now, Tuborg," said Miss Applebutter, "you must mind your manners. Our visitor was probably just expecting something…"

"Bigger," said the man, "much bigger. Mildred instructed me to come home with a pup, but this one could fit into my own palm. You sure you don't have one more in a larger size?"

"But I am a larger size," said Tuborg. "You just can't see it."

"I don't see it," said the large man, "but I am in desperate circumstances. Let's say we try this again. My name is Jack Kingsley and I'm in need of a dog. Now if Tuborg is all that you've got, well, maybe Tuborg is all that I need. You see, son, we don't need a lap dog. Me and Mildred already got one of those. What I want to do, son, is offer you a job."

"Me?" said Tuborg, excitably, wagging his little stump of a tail, "A job? This must be my lucky day. Well I accept your job, sir. I am your man!"

"Now you just wait right here, son," said Mr. Kingsley, "you haven't even heard what the job entails."

"Doesn't matter to me," said Tuborg. "I'm your man, sir. You can count on me."

"Well isn't he just an eager beaver," said Mr. Kingsley. "This boy's got spunk — if not size."

"He is spunky," said Miss Applebutter. "I'll give him that. But what is the job you speak of, sir, if I may ask?"

"Why, he's going to be our guard dog," replied Mr. Kingsley. "Tuborg will be the last line of defense for our home. You think you can handle that, son? It's quite a responsibility."

"I'm up for the challenge, sir. I'll gladly be your last line of defense."

"I must say, this boy does have grit," said Mr. Kinsgley. "I'll take him off your hands if you'll allow me, ma'am. I'll certainly give him a try."

Miss Applebutter and Mr. Kingsley exchanged pleasantries and finalized Tuborg's adoption. Mr. Kinglsey then gathered up Tuborg in his palm and took him out to his truck. They then roared away into the night.

Somewhere along the many miles Tuborg fell fast asleep. When he awoke, he was in a great big two-story home at the foot of a giant staircase. Tuborg gathered his senses and saw that Mr. Kingsley was standing right beside him. "Is this where you live?" asked Tuborg, rubbing his eyes awake.

"Why yes it is," replied Mr. Kingsley. "But Tuborg, this is where you live as well. We're home now, boy."

"Home?"

"Of course, home," said Mr. Kingsley. "Now it's time for you to meet the others."

"The others?" Tuborg gulped.

Just then, a woman in a flowing nightgown descended down the staircase. And in her arms was the most beautiful puppy Tuborg had ever laid his eyes on.

"Tuborg," said Mr. Kingsley, "this is my wife, Mildred, and this our other puppy, Cordelia."

"*Yowza*," muttered Tuborg.

"What's that you said, boy?" asked Mr. Kingsley. "I didn't quite catch that."

"I just said I'm pleased to you meet you, ma'am, and pleased to meet you too, Cordelia."

"That's what I thought you said," added Mr. Kingsley.

"I'm actually too young to date anyhow, sir. I meant no offense."

"I'm sure you are too young to date, boy. I'm sure that you are."

"Now Jack," said Mildred, "do you mean to tell me *this* is the guard dog you were told to bring home? How on earth is this little whippersnapper supposed to protect Cordelia and me?"

"Well, Mildred, I know Tuborg's got little britches to begin with, but I think in due time he'll grow into them. Don't you think so? Don't you think we ought to at least give him a try?"

Mildred bent down to kiss little Cordelia. "So little Cordi, do you think we ought to give the little fellow a try?"

Cordelia sniffed at the air but Tuborg couldn't tell at all what that meant. He hoped and prayed for the best. At length, Mildred looked down upon Tuborg. "Cordi says we'll give you a try, young man."

"Oh boy!" exclaimed Tuborg. "I won't let you down, ma'am. Not now or ever."

"He sure is a feisty one," said Mildred. "I'll give him that."

Mildred and Cordelia ascended up the stairs leaving Tuborg with Mr. Kingsley. When the ladies were out of earshot, Mr. Kingsley said to Tuborg, "We'll be sleeping upstairs and you'll be in charge of downstairs. It's a big area down here, Tuborg, so I want you to sleep with one eye open."

"Oh, I'll sleep with both eyes open, sir. You can count on me."

Mr. Kingsley showed Tuborg the first floor layout, then brought him into the kitchen for a midnight snack. He made a blanket bed in the corner for Tuborg and then went up the stairs to bed. He told Tuborg to be ready first thing in the morning, for his day on the job would be a long one. Tuborg tried his hardest to sleep with both eyes open, but one soon shut followed by the other and off to sleep he drifted. He was home now, and his sleep was warm and peaceful and deep…

At sunrise the next morning, Mr. Kingsley rousted Tuborg awake. After a quick breakfast, he led the little puppy out the back door. Tuborg gazed upon a wide, fenced-in lawn as green as he could ever imagine. There was one big oak tree smack in the middle of the grass, but that was it. "Tuborg," said Mr. Kingsley, "this is my backyard. I take good care of it and I'm mighty proud of the results."

"As you should be, sir."

"Now, Tuborg," Mr. Kingsley continued, "I'm gone an awful lot, and I don't have the time to watch over my land. That's where you come in. You see, your day job will be to guard this property, understand?"

"Yes, sir. I'll guard it all right. You can count on me."

"Nobody but me and Mildred and Cordelia comes and goes back here, understand?"

"I understand, sir," said Tuborg. "I'm ready to start at once, sir."

"That's good to hear, Tuborg. That's good to hear. Now I've got something for you to wear. I want you to look official and represent our family well."

Mr. Kingsley had a small box tucked under his arm. He placed it front of Tuborg and opened it.

"Is that what I think it is?" asked Tuborg, nervously.

"This here is the uniform I want you wear. You've got a blue shirt, a cap, and a badge."

"Oh boy! A uniform!"

"You wear it with pride, son."

Tuborg immediately slipped on the shirt and then placed the cap on his head. As he was fumbling with the badge, he said to Mr. Kingsley, "And will there be a gun and a holster as well?"

Mr. Kingsley held his big belly and laughed. "Now don't you get ahead of yourself, boy. You've got to walk before you can run if you know what I mean."

"Oh, I'll walk, sir. I'll walk every inch of this lawn a thousand times over. Nothing will ever get by old Tuborg. You can be sure of that."

"All right, all right," said Mr. Kingsley, bending over Tuborg and giving the puppy a friendly little pat. "I do believe I've got the right man for the job after all. Now I shall leave you to your work."

Tuborg did indeed walk every inch of the property within the big brown fences. Eventually he made his way to the oak tree in the middle. There he found a heart carved into the trunk. In the middle of the heart there was a scratching that read *J + M*. This is a good home, Tuborg thought to himself, with a good yard and a good tree. He would guard this place with everything he's got.

Tuborg noticed small things at first. The calm breeze, a darting squirrel, a screaming blue jay, a praying mantis. Nothing to cause alarm, nothing to investigate. But just as he backed up to the tree to settle in and take five, he heard what he thought was a knocking at the front fence. Tuborg rushed over to the fence and barked a strong warning. But when he got there he could see nothing between the slats of the fence. After a moment he turned away, sensing everything was on the up and up. But then he heard another knocking. What was going on? He could see nothing. Finally a voice came. "Hey, buddy, we're down here."

"Who's down here?" asked Tuborg.

"*We are*," said the voice. "We all are."

Tuborg bent his head lower, and sure enough there was a tiny gate at the bottom of the fence, no more than an inch or two high. Tuborg worked his paw to open the gate a crack. What he saw was amazing. It was a tiny man in a uniform, but not a uniform like his own. He was a marching band leader, and behind him a band of over a hundred strong hoisting musical instruments of every kind imaginable. "My gosh, you're the biggest dog I think I've ever seen," said the band leader.

"I am?" questioned Tuborg. "But I'm the runt of the litter. You should see my brothers and sisters."

"If they're larger than you are," said the band leader, "then I don't ever want to see your brothers and sisters."

Tuborg smiled. He was finally big — at least compared to the marching band before him.

"Now sonny, you've got to let us cross your yard," said the band leader. "We're very late."

"But I can't let you cross the yard. Mr. Kingsley forbids it."

"Yes," said the band leader, "but does Mr. Kingsley know that blue team is playing the red team and it's the biggest game of the season? Now what would the biggest game of the season be without a marching band?"

"I see your point," said Tuborg, rubbing his chin. "He didn't tell me anything about the big game."

"No, he didn't. But don't you worry. We won't cause a ruckus. We'll just play our tunes and march right across the yard and out the back door. It's all standard procedure for marching bands. That's right. All standard procedure."

"Well, if it's standard procedure…"

"In fact," said the band leader, "I'll even give you my baton and you can lead them through. How about that?"

"Wow!" said Tuborg. "Me, a band leader? Imagine that."

"There's nothing to imagine, sonny. This is the real deal. Lead them through!"

Tuborg held the baton high and led the marching band all the way across the yard to the back of the fence. Sure enough there was another tiny door to let the band out. He surrendered the baton to the band leader and shut the little door. And then they were gone. It was Mildred's voice he heard next. Tuborg ran back to the house so he could better hear her.

"Tuborg, what is all that noise I'm hearing?" asked Mildred.

"Oh nothing, ma'am. It's just the wind is all."

"Well, the wind sure does sound like *When the Saints Go Marching In.*"

"It's a very nice wind you've got back here, ma'am," said Tuborg.

"Well, tell the wind to keep it down, okay?"

"Yes, ma'am. I will."

Tuborg took a few laps around the perimeter of the yard to make sure everything was kosher, then settled down to take five against the tree. But as soon as he plopped his butt on the ground there came another rapping at the gate. Tuborg barked a stern warning and dashed over as quickly as he could. Now what, he thought, bending his ear down to the little door. "Open up!" he heard. "The circus is in town."

Tuborg timidly propped open the door. "The circus?"

A tiny man in a sharp tuxedo and a tall top hat emerged from behind the door. In his hand he waved a baton and smiled as brightly as one could. "My gosh, look at the size of you," he said to Tuborg. "Are you some kind of polar bear?"

"A polar bear, me?" said Tuborg. "No, sir, I'm just a guard dog."

"A guard dog, huh?" said the tiny man. "What's your name?"

"I'm Tuborg."

"Well, Mr. Tuborg, I do believe you're the fiercest, roughest, toughest guard dog I ever did lay eyes on."

"I am?" replied Tuborg, puffing out his chest.

"But I sense that you're a reasonable dog as well."

"I'd like to think so, sir," said Tuborg. "But what about you? Who are you?"

"Why Mr. Tuborg, I'm the Ringmaster, the master of ceremonies, the talk of the town, the baron of the big top, the biggest of the big!"

"You're all of those things?" said Tuborg. "Wow."

The Ringmaster propped open the door as wide as he could manage. Behind the door was a long line of every kind of circus performer there was. There were jugglers, trapeze artists, tight rope walkers, fire eaters, men and women on stilts, and more. "Now as you can see, son, the circus is in town. Now you've got to let us through. We're late for our show and time's a wasting. You don't want the children to miss out on the circus, do you?"

"But I just let a marching band cross the yard," explained Tuborg. "How can I let the circus come through, too? You want to get me fired?"

"Mr. guard dog," said the Ringmaster, "what do you see at the point of my baton?"

"Well," said Tuborg, "I see five clowns."

"What you see, son, is five *sad* clowns. Now you've got to help us turn those frowns upside down."

"How do I do that?" asked Tuborg.

"By letting us pass, by letting us cross the yard," said the Ringmaster. "That's how. Don't you love a clown?"

"Well, to be honest…"

All of the sudden the clowns started crying and moaning. "Now look what you've done, son. I've got five crying clowns on my hands. Who doesn't love a clown I say?"

"All right, all right," said Tuborg. "I'll let you pass. I sure don't want to see anyone in tears, certainly not five clowns."

"That's my boy!" said the Ringmaster, ushering the once again happy clowns back into formation. "And as for your reward, here is my baton. You, Tuborg, are the honorary leader of the circus, the temporary Ringmaster who looks like a polar bear. Take us through, son!"

Tuborg grabbed the little baton and led the long column of circus performers across the yard and out the back gate. With all of their musical instruments and clowning, the circus made quite a commotion. Tuborg was very glad when the last of them passed through the gate. Once they were gone, however, he heard the voice of Mildred. This time she was out on the back porch — with Cordelia by her side. "Tuborg!" she called from across the yard. "Is there something amiss in the yard?"

"No, ma'am," Tuborg called as he ran toward them. "We're all clear back here."

Mildred held up her hand to stop a running Tuborg dead in his tracks. "Why do I smell peanuts then?"

"Oh, they're in season, ma'am. It's definitely high peanut season I believe."

"And you're a farmer as well, Tuborg?" said Mildred.

"It sure smells like the circus," said Cordelia, gazing upon Tuborg with a suspicious eye. "It most surely does."

Tuborg felt it was best to hold his tongue. Anything else he said might make it worse. Mildred took a look around the yard and made sure the coast was clear. "Now, Tuborg, the real reason we've come out here is because Cordelia needs to go potty. What I need you to do is be a gentleman and face the opposite direction from where she goes. A lady needs her privacy, understand?"

"Oh yes, ma'am," said Tuborg. "I'll bury my head in the ground if that's what it takes."

"Well aren't you the little gentleman," said Mildred. "It's nice to have a gentleman in the house."

"It's part of my job," replied Tuborg, "and a lifestyle choice as well."

"My, my, Tuborg," said Mildred, patting him on his cap "aren't you scoring points with me today!"

Cordelia came running back, eventually going back inside the house with Mildred. Tuborg himself went potty, and then settled down under the tree for an afternoon nap. He was awakened not much later by another knocking at the gate. "What now?" Tuborg said, rousing himself from a deep slumber. "Not another circus I hope." He trotted over to the tiny door and crouched down low. "Who goes there?" he asked.

"Howdy, pardner!" called a booming voice. "Open the door! Let me see your peepers."

"My peepers?" questioned Tuborg.

"Your eyes," said the voice. "I want to meet you face to face."

Tuborg tentatively opened the door. On the other side he found a tiny cowboy wearing boots and spurs, dirty jeans, and a ten-gallon hat. "Friends call me Tex," he said, doffing his hat. And behind Tex were four other mini cowboys, and then a head of tiny cattle as far as he could see.

"What the..?" exclaimed Tuborg.

"Pleased to meet you, friend," said Tex. "What's your name?"

"I'm Tuborg, the guard dog for this yard. What are you doing with all this cattle?"

"Well," said Tex, "we're on a cattle drive as you can see. We've got to drive this cattle because that's what we do. We drive them here, and then we turn around and drive them there. Now if you'll kindly let us cross your land, we'll be out of your hair in no time. By the way, you're about the biggest varmint I ever did see. What did you say your name was again, Bullfrog?"

"The name is *Tuborg*. Now why should I let you cross our yard? You could get me in big trouble."

"I'd say trouble is your middle name."

"It's not," replied Tuborg. "It's Joseph."

"Well, Tuborg Joseph, I've got a deal for you. You let us cross the yard, and I'll let you lead the rooty-tootyest cattle drive you ever did see. Are you ready to be a cowboy, Bullfrog?"

"Oh, brother," sighed Tuborg, propping open the door as far as he could. "All right, cowboys, line them up. I'll take you through. Yee-ha!"

Tuborg led the cowboys and the cattle in a straight line across the yard. He let them out on the other side. "Whew," he said, dusting off his shirt, "what a day."

Soon after, Mr. Kingsley appeared at the back porch. He called for Tuborg across the yard. The little guard dog ran as fast as he could to the back porch. Mr. Kingsley let his eyes gaze upon the large expanse of his yard. "Looks awfully dusty back here, Tuborg. What do you think?"

"We just haven't had the rains this year, sir."

"No," replied Mr. Kingsley, "we sure have not. Now tell me about your first day, Tuborg. Anything of note to report?"

"No, sir. It's all jake back here, sir."

"All jake? Is that right? Well, Tuborg, then let's get you some supper. Looks like you've well deserved it."

Mr. Kingsley attempted to usher Tuborg inside, but the little dog wouldn't budge. 'What's the matter, Tuborg? Ain't you hungry?"

"I am, sir," admitted Tuborg, "very hungry. But I have to tell you something. I cannot tell a lie."

"What lie is that, son?"

"That everything was jake. No, sir, everything wasn't jake. It wasn't jake at all. In fact, there were breaches."

"Breaches!" Mr. Kingsly exclaimed. "There were breaches in my backyard?"

"Three of them actually," replied Tuborg.

"Three breaches you say? What kind of three breaches?"

"Well, first there was a tiny marching band, a hundred of them, but no more than an inch high. But, you see, the red team was playing the blue team and they really needed a marching band to play. They couldn't be late for a game like that."

"That is true," admitted Mr. Kingsley. "The red team did play the blue team, and it sure wouldn't have been the same without a marching band. Now tell me about the second breach."

"Next there was a mini circus. The clowns were crying and they didn't want to let the little children down. They couldn't have been late for the big show."

"I don't suppose not," said Mr. Kingsley. "Nobody likes a clown… I mean, a crying clown. A crying clown will bring you down. That's what I always say."

"Me too, sir," said Tuborg. "Me too."

"Now tell me about this third breach."

"They were tiny cowboys, sir, real ones, but tiny, and a herd of tiny cattle as far as you can see…"

"All right, all right, Tuborg," said Mr. Kingsley, laughing. "Let's go inside and get us some supper. I want to hear all about the cowboys, the cattle, the circus. In fact, I want to hear about everything…"

Tuborg had supper with his new family and told them all about his adventures in the backyard. In the next days and weeks he settled into his job as guard dog. He did continue to let some groups cross the yard. The marching bands and circuses and cattle drives came and went, as did a dancing troupe, some Girl Scouts, a lacrosse team, and a comedian named Marty. He did not, however, let in zombies, litterbugs, solicitors, or anyone Mr. Kingsley considered tumbleweeds, turnip seeds, hockey pucks, flimflammers, sidewinders, gullywumpers, rabblerousers, and an especially heinous group calling themselves *The Brigade of Angry Cats.*

In time, Mr. Kingsley led Tuborg out to the big tree. There they carved out a new heart right next to the one that read *J + M.* In it, Mr. Kingsley helped Tuborg carve out *T + C.* In the big house, with the big yard, and a big tree in the middle, they lived happily ever after.

The Man Who Lost His Cheese

Where is my cheese?
Where has it gone?
I just want my cheese
back where it belongs.

Did you steal my cheese?
Did you make it go?
I really miss my cheese.
I just wanted you to know.

Bring me back my cheese.
We both know it's you.
Bring me back my cheese.
I'm feeling so blue.

If you return my cheese,
I promise I'll share.
If you return my cheese,
True love I'll declare.

Won't you return my cheese?
Won't you return it, please?
Oh, my cheese! My dear, dear cheese!
Where have you gone?

Printed in the United States
By Bookmasters